AT LEAST HE'S NOT ON FIRE:

A Tour of the Things That Escape My Head

Chris Philbrook

At Least He's Not on Fire: A Tour of the Things That Escape My Head
Copyright © 2010 Christopher Philbrook

All rights reserved. No part of this book may be reproduced or transmitted in any form or by any means, electronic or mechanical, including photocopying, recording, or any information storage and retrieval system, without prior written permission of the author. Your support of author's rights is appreciated.

Published in the United States of America

First Publishing Date October, 2010

All characters in this compilation are fictitious. Any resemblance to actual persons, living or dead, is purely coincidental.

Cover illustration by Ian Llanas

Design and interior layout by Alan MacRaffen

This book is dedicated to the thousands of people who have parted ways with their time and money to get their hands on the words that have slipped free of my imagination, and are now running amok inside yours.

-Chris

Also by Chris Philbrook:

<u>Elmoryn - The Kinless Trilogy</u>
Book One: Wrath of the Orphans
Book Two: The Motive for Massacre

Coming Soon:
Book Three: The Echoes of Sin

<u>Reemergence</u>
Tesser: A Dragon Among Us

<u>Adrian's Undead Diary</u>
Book One: Dark Recollections
Book Two: Alone No More
Book Three: Midnight
Book Four: The Failed Coward
Book Five: Wrath
Book Six: In the Arms of Family
Book Seven: The Trinity

Coming Soon:
Book Eight: Cassie

Welcome to At Least He's Not on Fire

Hey folks. I'm Chris. Thanks for taking the time to buy or borrow and then theoretically read this book or part thereof. Frightening isn't it? Trying to get inside the mind of a stranger. I'm sure by now you're thinking to yourself; do I have enough coffee or beer or tea to make it through a decent reading session? If you don't go ahead and set this down and take care of yourself. Go pee too if you have to.

Done? Excellent. Now the scary part: the stories.

At Least He's Not on Fire *serves a big purpose for me. I write a lot of stuff, and getting that stuff out to as large an audience as possible is tough in this day and age. The market is saturated with self published authors (some great, some good, and some... who should be working on coloring books) and to stand out in the crowd you need lots of reviews, and lots of opportunities to be discovered. This book is another way for me to be discovered.*

This book also serves as a way for me to share some stories I've written that don't have a proper home, and also as a way to thank my existing reader base. If you're new; welcome to the world of my writing. If you're already a fan of my writing and you're reading this anyway; you rock. I mean that. Every review you write, every person you talk about my books to, and every little message you send my way helps me in some way or another. You are making my dreams come true, and that is NOT a little thing.

At Least He's Not on Fire *has a bunch of stuff in it. There's a table of contents in a page or so that'll lay it all out for you. There's enormous variety in my writing. If you read and dislike one thing, try something else. There's a really good chance you'll like a different story. What's weird is if you like one thing, there's a good chance you'll like it all. It's weird like that.*

Or you won't like any of it. If that's the case, you can put the book down, no real skin off your back.

However... I did steal some of your life, and that's like

winning for me.

Enjoy this book. Writing the contents of it has been a huge pleasure for me, and I'm excited to share all of my work, old and new, with friends old and new. Trying to be a writer is the hardest work I've ever loved.

Also, here's a mad shout out to Ian Llanas, the dude who did the cover for this. Loved working with him, and I love the final product. Good on you sir.

Chris Philbrook
Hillsboro NH, April of 2014

Table of Contents:

All In 13

    Preview:
Adrian's Undead Diary 29

Hell Hole 57

    Preview:
Tesser: A Dragon Among Us
    A Reemergence Novel 71

The Vampire of Menlo Park 105

    Preview:
The Wrath of the Orphans
    Book One of The Kinless Trilogy 127

About the Author 214

Additional Online Content 215

All In

I wrote All In *as a submission to an anthology a couple of years ago. When I submitted it, I was real proud of it, and like every other writer in the world, I KNEW it was going to be picked up.*

It wasn't.

I shared it as a premium short story over on adriansundeaddiary.com and the folks there said nice things about it. I pulled it up for this project and edited the crap out of it. Added over a thousand words, and fleshed it out to be a little creepier, and a bit funnier. With all the additional work put into it, it's far better now.

A hand of cards with the Devil? Might win a pot of things you don't want.

Enjoy.

"So have you ever actually been to Georgia?" Wallace asked the Devil.

Sitting across the card table from Wallace, riffle shuffling the deck between the two of them the Devil cracked a wide, evil grin. He could appreciate the humor in the joke. "Oh Wally. What a charming question that is. I've never heard *that* one before. I'll answer that and the next one, free of charge. I most certainly have been to Georgia, and I can play mean fiddle to boot."

Wallace's blood ran cold. He suddenly wished he'd never

opened his mouth after losing a hand at this very table earlier. The casino both figures—man and greatest power of evil—sat alone in at the moment, had emptied in the snap of a finger the moment Wallace threw his hands up in the air, and yelled at the top of his lungs, "What, do I have to sell my soul for a fucking pair here?!"

It was his worst mistake ever, Wallace had decided, and that was saying something. A failed marriage, a thirteen year old in rehab, and a car probably being repossessed in the parking lot as he played were just the recent mistakes he'd made. After his exclamation, blood boiling, Wallace looked back down from the ornate pressed-tin ceiling of the gambling house. Everyone had disappeared into thin air, and the dark lord of night himself had appeared across the green felt card table. Wallace didn't need to ask him who he was, or what he was there for. A thousand people don't just disappear in Vegas, leaving their drinks and their chips behind unless the one dollar buffet had just opened.

Wallace was sure the buffet was closed.

The Devil looked clean, smooth, and handsome. In a different light, on a different day, he could've easily been on the cover of a fashion magazine instead of being the leader of the legions of Hell. He had dark, smooth skin the color of pressed and refined olive oil. His hair was short, cut in the style of the 50's, swept back, and glistened like it was made from strands of obsidian. The subtle red pinstripes on his black suit played with Wallace's eyes. The thin crimson stripes shifted and ebbed as if he had lava just below the surface of the fabric. Heat waves emanated from his shoulders and shimmered into nothing as they rose toward the lights and cameras above. His eyes matched his tie, both scarlet red like the blood presently running cold in Wallace's veins.

"Wally please. Don't stare. It's very rude of you. You act like you've never seen evil before." The Devil's voice was sultry, and had an accent that he couldn't place.

Maybe that's a total lack of an accent, Wally thought

suddenly. *Evil doesn't have a nationality.*

"What's the game going to be Wally? Blackjack? Five card stud? Goldfish? I've always been partial to Omaha, despite what you might've heard elsewhere." The Devil's fingers danced over the deck of cards, splitting, shuffling and doing it again like a machine powered by centuries of honed evil grace. Every card moved to his finger's will without hesitation. Wally's eyes were fixated as the red backed cards moved in the Devil's long, sinister digits.

"Well, I uh, I was thinking maybe I'd just, you know, maybe cut my losses and call it a night. I'm out of chips anyway so maybe I'll just be going, if you don't mind." Wally pushed the plush leather chair back from the poker table and started to stand. He thought of his son in Malibu, trying to flush the heroin out of his body. Wally had to get back. To see him. Squeeze him, and tell him his father loved him very much, and maybe, to apologize for being such a shitty father for so long. Wally just needed to get out of the casino...

The Devil's words stopped him like a statue, "I do mind Wallace. I mind very much. I've come all this way, and taken the time out of my very busy schedule to offer you a fair game of chance for what you've asked for, and I won't leave without at least *one* hand. Sit. Play. After all I've done for you it's the least you can do for me." The Devil never stopped shuffling. His eyes pointed at the seat Wally had just vacated.

Wallace swallowed hard and slid back down into the chair. The worn leather creaked against his weight as he pulled himself back up to the table's edge. The Devil presented the deck in the middle of the table like a sacrificial dagger on an altar. He sat up straight and interlaced his long fingers. Wally was reminded of a bat folding itself up in leathery black wings.

"I could maybe play a hand of hold 'em," Wally offered meekly.

The Devil's eyed flared like coals hit with a gust from the

bellows. "Oh *could* you Wally? Just one hand for little old me? That would just make my day. *Cut the deck.*" The Devil lowered his eyes and stared intently at the cards. Wally's trembling hand brushed across the soft green felt and cut the deck in half. He sat the top of the deck beside the bottom, and took his hand away quickly. The cards were warm to the touch.

Of their own accord the thin cards reassembled into a single cohesive pile and began to fly across the table, dispensing hands. One went to Wally, then the Devil, and then again until two cards sat in front of both players. Wally stared down at the two cards as if they were poisonous to the touch. The Devil reached down and scooped his two cards up eagerly, holding them up close to his face so that only his red eyes peered out above them. The Devil looked at his cards, and lowered them to the table face down, revealing a smile filled with pearly white teeth. For a moment, Wally thought he saw a speck of flesh stuck between two of the incisors.

"Well, aren't you going to look?" The Devil wagged a finger at the cards sitting in front of Wally. Wally licked his lips nervously and lowered one sweaty hand to them, eventually lifting one card by its edge, like a child peering under an old board in the woods that a spider might be underneath. Wally glanced down and saw it was the ace of hearts.

"Wait, we totally forgot the wager!" The Devil leaned forward in his chair across the table until he seemed to be right in Wally's face. Wally's nose caught the foul odor of brimstone. "It seems as if though we've already looked at our cards, which is very much not normal. However, perhaps we can make a game within a game out of it? What do you say Wally?"

The image of the ace of hearts sat in the back of Wally's mind like a brick of solid gold. The power of the ace in poker was nearly unmatched, and knowing he had one gave him a thrill. He tried to hide his situation by reminding himself he was playing the Devil. "I'm listening."

"Excellent, I knew you were a good sport!" The Devil sat back and tapped his chin with a slender finger, thinking. After a moment, his eyes flared mischievously, and he smiled once more. "I'll let you choose your fate Wally. How's that?"

"I'm still listening." Wally's confidence was growing every second. HIs ace felt like, well, an ace in the hole for him.

"If you place your bet before you look at that other card, I'll agree that if you win, you get to keep your soul, and I'll see to it that you win every pot for the rest your life. If you look at that second card before you bet, then your soul is still on the line, and if you win, you just get to keep your soul. No cash prizes as well. Sound fair?"

Wally ran the numbers. He calculated all the odds of what hands could beat him, and decided that if he was going to put his soul on the line, he might as well get something for it if he won. He could pay for his son's rehab, and bank a few year's worth of child support payments all at once.

"One card it is, I'm all in." Wally reached down and flipped his two cards over. The ace of hearts came to a rest with the six of diamonds on top of it. Wally's heart sank like a stone in quicksand. Starting with an ace there was little he would want less than a six that was off suited. It wasn't a heart like his ace, nor was it low enough to help make a straight using that ace. He was reduced to riding the power of the ace alone, hoping another six came down to pair with his six, or pray that enough cards to make a straight somehow appeared.

Once again it seemed like Wally needed a pair. He knew for certain he could get a pair for his soul now, but that seemed very insufficient at the moment.

"Mmmmmm..." the Devil looked as satisfied like a cat with a feather poking out of its mouth. "Oh that ace lured you in, didn't it? What a shame. All the glitz and glamour of that single, solitary red heart Wally. Gets 'em every time," the Devil said with a curling smile, and Wally knew his time was short unless he got very lucky.

The Devil leaned back in the leather casino chair and with a flourish flipped and placed his two cards on the Kelly green felt. The six of clubs and the six of spades sat there on the table, practically mocking poor Wally.

"I should've known three sixes would come down. I mean, it's you, right? Fitting." Wally smirked at the Devil. He was fucked and he knew it. For once, he didn't think of his own fate. He thought of his boy growing up without a father. Well, his boy finishing growing up without a father.

The Devil nodded knowingly as if any other possibility was impossible. "If I'm going to do it, might as well be thematic about it. I'm a sucker for good drama Wally."

"Well, let's see the flop, get this over with," Wally said with a dejected sigh. He had resigned to his fate.

"As you wish Wally." The Devil wiggled his fingers casually in the air as if he were manipulating a marionette. In response, the top card of the deck lifted itself into the air and burst into flames, incinerating with a puff of black smoke. In slow motion the top three cards peeled off the top of the deck, rotated face up, and came to a rest three abreast. They could've been dealt by a ghost.

The king of spades, jack of clubs, and ten of hearts.

Wally's heart raced as his mind assembled the puzzle. With his ace he could make a straight if a queen came down on either of the next two cards. If another ace came out his pair would beat the Devil's pair of sixes. The Devil's hand was still winning, but Wally had several outs, and his soul was not lost yet. A tiny bit of hope crept into him again. It felt like finding a twenty in a jacket you hadn't worn since the last winter.

"Wally. Look at you, playing Yahtzee during a poker game. How lucky can a man be? You think that magical ace or queen is going to come down against me? I'm the Lord of Darkness Wally, seriously." The Devil arched an eyebrow and looked at Wally incredulously, taunting him.

AT LEAST HE'S NOT ON FIRE

Wally shrugged at the Devil and leaned onto the table. "I'm all in anyway Mr. Devil. Flip the cards and get this over with. I've got places to go and I'm feeling lucky."

The Devil smiled. "Mr. Devil? So formal. Wally you can call me Mr. Scratch if you like, or Nick. I feel like we're on a first name basis now."

Wally smirked. He had to admit the fucker was charming.

The Devil waggled his fingers once more and the top card levitated up, and burst into flames. The card below flipped over and came to rest beside the first three.

The six of hearts.

Wally leaned back in his chair and let his head flop backwards in disgust. Old Nick was up to no good, it was obvious now. Trip sixes for the Devil meant Wally's chance at keeping his soul had plummeted. Eyes staring at the baroque patterns etched into the metallic ceiling, Wally heard the Devil laugh. It reminded him of a broken church organ, off key, grating on the ears as well as the soul he was about to lose. When Wally finally tilted his head up and back to the table, the Devil was sipping on a glass of thick, dark fluid. It could've been motor oil.

"Thirsty?" the Devil asked him. "Might want to hydrate while you have the chance Wally." The Devil smiled, holding his tumbler up in a mock toast.

"Kiss my ass," Wally spat at him. "You're a dirty cheat."

"Again with the rudeness Wally. And you haven't even lost yet. You've still got a sporting chance here!" The Devil slowly twirled his glass, clinking the ice cubes floating in the greasy fluid.

"Do it, come on." Wally closed his eyes and tapped his fingers on the table, cascading the fingertips from left to right and back again, hoping his luck would finally rise to the top. In the back of his mind he said a short prayer to a God he rarely leaned on. There was some regret in that part of his mind.

"As you wish, Wally."

Wally couldn't see what was happening through his shut eyelids, but he sensed the first card move into the air, and heard the poomph when it burst into flames. In his mind's eye he envisioned the next card, the final card of the hand, slide off the top of the deck and come to a rest next to the six of hearts.

Silence.

"Hm." He heard the Devil mutter. "Well Wally, don't you want to see your fate? This seems like the kind of thing you might want to aim your eyeballs at."

Wally envisioned a queen, any queen in his mind. He slowly cracked his eyelids and peered out at the Devil's face. The Devil's eyes were locked on the fifth and final card of the game. Wally's line of sight slowly slid downward, following the line the Devil's eyes took.

The queen of hearts was the fifth card. Wally had made his straight.

"WOOO! WOOO!" Wally leapt up out of the chair, shaking the card table and sending the cracked leather chair flying backwards. He pumped his fist and walked in circles, yelling at the top of his lungs. "I beat the Devil baby! Yeah! I'm the MAN! FUCK YEAH!"

The Devil sat emotionless at the table, watching his failed prey celebrate the victory. After watching Wally for as long as he could stand, the Devil spoke up, "Wally."

Wally froze at the sound of the Devil's cold voice. He spun and looked at Mr. Scratch, an expression on his face that looked as if he'd been caught with his hands in the cookie jar. "Yeah?"

"Congratulations." The Devil nodded his head, showing respect to Wally.

"Thanks. So I win every pot for the rest of my life now? No matter what?" Wally was starting to get giddy just thinking about what he could win. Cars, fame, women, all of it was just a wager away. The thoughts of paying child support, and covering the crushing cost of his son's rehabilitation had slipped into the ether.

AT LEAST HE'S NOT ON FIRE

The Devil's response was flat, devoid of emotion. That scared Wally more than the Devil's earlier gloating. "Every hand Wally. Winnah winnah, chicken dinnah. What say we go double or nothing? Make this interesting? One more hand?"

Wally's color drained away. He had everything he wanted already, why risk it? He'd beaten the Devil, and would now win every pot for the rest of his life? Why bother risking it? "What's in it for me? I've already got what I want. And if I win everything else from here on out I won't want for a damned thing."

"Mmm. Greed. I like it. Let's say if you win this one, I'll guarantee you get a free pass with the big guy, and the pearly gates open as wide as can be at the end of your days, no matter what. And if I win, well, let's just say your soul goes back on the block." The Devil's eyebrows danced up and down flirtatiously. Once again the Devil interlaced his fingers, and Wally was reminded of those leathery wings cocooning around a chunk of coal, a nugget of purest evil.

Wally considered it, and then abruptly picked his knocked over chair up off the empty casino floor. "Alright, let's do this. I got this. I beat you once, I can beat you again."

A slow insidious smile crept across the Devil's face as Wally pulled up to the card table once more, "Arrogance too Wally? You spoil me. This is like that birthday holiday you all celebrate in December."

"Don't get used to it. I won't be here long."

"Of that I am sure Wally. Shall we?" The Devil's hands came apart and the deck on the table began shuffling itself. The Devil's fiery eyes were locked on Wally's, and this time, Wally didn't look away.

"Whoa. Wait a damn second. New deck there Mr. Scratch. All fifty two cards. No cheating," Wally said as he shook his head, giving the Devil a dirty look.

"Oh my, I had totally forgotten." The Devil said with feigned guilt in his voice. He waved his hands and the deck disappeared with a puff of smoke. He reached inside his suit and produced a new deck. Wally noticed the glow of embers peek out when the suit opened.

The new deck, possibly fresh from a printing press in Hell itself came to life in the Devil's hands. His dagger like fingers split the cards, shuffled them, and did it again. After a multitude of shuffles the Devil sat the deck down again, slowly pushing it to Wally. He tilted his hand, offering the cut to the man.

With no tremble this time Wally reached out and cut the deck in half. He picked up the second half and placed it on the first. The warmth of the cards was there again, but it didn't frighten Wally. Wally was positive he had this game in the bag. He was sure of it.

The Devil's eyes narrowed as Wally sat back confidently. "Ready Wally? Double or nothing, remember?"

"Yeah you bet, let's do this." Wally waved a dismissive hand at the Devil.

The Devil made an annoyed face, and sucked on his gleaming white teeth. He raised his long fingers again, and the cards flew to their proper places in front of the two players, man, and evil.

"All in." Wally didn't even glance down at his cards. He looked the Devil in the flaming eyes and put on his stone cold poker expression. No emotion, no thoughts, just confidence.

"Interesting. I suppose I'll take that bet. Double or nothing Wally, flip 'em." The Devil reached down and flipped over his cards, and Wally did the same.

In front of the Devil was the ace of spades, and the king of spades, a powerful hand that was nearly unbeatable. Wally nodded in approval and looked down at his own cards. His hand consisted of the seven of clubs, and the two of diamonds.

"Hahahaha!" The Devil roared in laughter. He spread his arms wide, making clenched fists in triumph. Wally watched the Devil celebrate and had to blink to clear his eyes. He thought for a moment a pair of giant wings had sprouted out of the pinstriped suit. His eyes cleared, he saw he was in error. No wings were there.

"Come on Nick. I got things to do. Let's see these cards." Wally picked at his front teeth with his fingernail, illustrating how unimpressed he was with the Devil's hand.

"Oh Wally, you gloated when you won, spare me a little joy over this dramatic turn of events, yes?" The Devil leaned forward, a Cheshire grin spreading on his face.

Wally ignored the sinister King of Demons. "You haven't won anything yet. Let's do this."

The Devil's nose wrinkled, as he barely contained his impulse of fury at the insolence Wally was sending his way now. The Lord of Darkness had little patience for pricks like Wally. However, a deal is a deal, and Old Scratch was pot committed. The Devil tugged at the air, and as if it were connected to an invisible string, the top card flew off the deck, immolating itself. Before the puff of smoke had dissipated into the casino ceiling, the next three cards were flat on the table, revealing the developing hand.

Wally leaned over the table, clearly not surprised by what had come down. The Devil looked to Wally's face and saw the lack of alarm. The Devil's eyes, full of restrained rage, darted down and analyzed the cards.

The two of clubs, the seven of hearts, and the seven of diamonds appeared. The Devil's upper lip twitched. His nose wrinkled once more in disgust. The Devil was being betrayed by Lady Luck. Normally she was in his corner.

"Do you wanna fold? Or do you want to take this all the way out to the bitter end Nick?" Wally asked the Devil in a smarmy tone. The Devil's eyes shot back up to Wally's, glowing red like oven coils. Wally recoiled from the heat.

"This seems... unfair Wallace. At the very least I suspect you may have cheated me. There are grave consequences for cheating the Prince of Darkness you know." The Devil dragged his fingernails across the felt, ripping rents in the green fabric as easily as tearing tissue.

"Nah, nope. I'm playing by your rules. Your fault on this.

Flip the next two, you'll see." Wally pointed a finger at the deck, all the while staring at the growing black talons erupting from the end of the Devil's long fingertips. The olive skin was splitting apart around the nail bloodlessly, like clay cracking in the heat.

"As you wish Wallace." The Devil's voice had changed. It had gotten deeper. Wally noticed the Devil's canine teeth had grown, and his jaw seemed to be jutting out. The pinstripes on the suit had gotten wider as well, as if the suit was now being stretched apart by the wearer.

The Devil looked back to the deck and in rapid succession the top card burned into ash, a second card came out, another burst into flames, and the final card came after. The entire hand had been revealed.

"Haha, look at that." Wally laughed and pointed at the remaining cards on the table.

The Devil grunted and turned his head downwards to the cards. Wally noticed his forehead seemed shiny, and the skin tight. He noticed two bumps growing near the temples, just above the brow and pressing their way up through the skin. It looked quite painful to Wally.

The final two cards of the Devil's poker game were the remaining seven in the deck, and the two of hearts. Once again Wally had defeated the Devil at his own game.

"Take your pick, you can choose to lose to sevens full of deuces, or deuces full of sevens. Full house Devil, I win. I told you."

The skin stretched across the Devil's forehead popped with a ripping sound as two black horns pierced the flesh like curved obsidian stalagmites. They grew to a foot's length in the blink of an eye as the Devil bared a mouth filled with razor sharp yellowed teeth. His pearly whites were long gone.

"I... do *not* understand. You should have lost." The demonic face of the evolving, mutating Devil still had the capacity to show confusion. He looked left and right at the cards arrayed in front of him, trying to make sense of how he'd lost.

Wally leaned forward, almost apologetic in his approach. "Look, you TOLD me I'd win every pot I played until I died if I won that first hand. I won the first hand, and this was the next hand. You told me I'd win. The Devil's in the details man, of all people to remember that, I would've thought it would be you."

The Devil's body exploded in crimson light, forcing Wally to shield his eyes. His forearm was bright red from the heat when he pulled it away and looked. The Devil had returned to his pinstripe suit wearing, dashingly handsome prior form. Presently he had both hands on his stomach, and was letting loose a laugh that shook the chandeliers in the casino. Wally didn't know what to make of the situation, so he joined in on the Devil's self deprecating laughter.

"So I did Wallace, so I did. You know, I must be getting rusty. This is the third one of these I've muffed this week. Man that's frustrating. You people are getting clever. Too much cable television maybe." The Devil smiled, and shook his head at his own folly.

"Yeah well Nick, I guess you can't win them all, right?" Wally shrugged, offering up some comfort to Lucifer.

"Haha.. No Wally I guess not. Doesn't matter if I stack the deck sometimes or not. Good times Wallace. Oh hey, you know what's funny about all this?" The Devil asked, half in a laugh.

"What?" Wally asked through a smile.

"I said you'd win every pot for the rest of your life, right? Hahahaha…" The Devil's laughter was barely contained. Wally was reminded of when he was a young kid, and he came down with a case of the late night giggles. His mom used to call them "Wallygigglefits."

"Yeah, and I plan on using that prize to gain fame, and fortune. I'm going to pay for my kid's drug rehab too, and bank some child support payments to get that bitch off my back. You also said that if I won this second hand, I'd get into Heaven too, no questions asked." Wally sighed in appreciation of this tremendous victory over the Devil, and over evil. His life had finally taken the turn for the better he knew he deserved.

Absent of laughter, the Devil said, "Yeah, well, I'm a poor loser Wally. Plus I never said how many pots you'd have the chance to play. Have fun in Heaven. I'm gonna swing by Malibu and say hi to your kid on the way home."

Wally looked down at the Devil just as his head came off his shoulders.

The Devil watched Wally's head roll away down the casino aisle between the roulette tables and the craps tables. It bobbled sideways several times, and spun in a circle until it came to a rest against a velvet rope stand. Wally's eyes were stuck wide open, staring back at the Devil in shock. Lucifer stood up and licked the warm red blood off his hand like an infernal cat. Once he was clean of Wally's vitae, he adjusted his blood red tie, and walked away.

"Can't win 'em all is right Wallace. A lesson I wish I could learn."

Adrian's Undead Diary

When I was growing up in rural New Hampshire, my friends and I used to spend lots and lots of time doing three things; adventuring in the woods, playing Dungeons and Dragons, and watching the original zombie movies that kick started the genre.

When we weren't rolling dice, or going on long expeditions into the woods in search of adventure, we'd stay up late into the wee hours, hatching our plans in the event the apocalypse via zombie came into reality. I cannot emphasize how many hours we poured into these plans. To say they were extensive would be an epic understatement. These are some of my fondest memories and I'd relive them in a heartbeat if I could.

Joe, one of my best friends (and still one of my best friends, going on 25 years later) loved my ability to be a dungeon master and loved the silly short stories I wrote for creative writing class, and he begged me for years to write a story about all of our old zombie survival plans. "Do it," he said a thousand times, mimicking a goon from Goodfellas.

In the summer of 2010 I had a chance meeting with the godfather of the zombie craze at Rock N Shock in Massachusetts; George Romero. Ten minutes with George was one of the coolest things I've ever been able to do, and when I left the show that day I said to myself, "Self, write Joe that story. If George and friends can do it, so can you." I won't tell you about how I pulled up my shorts to show him a tattoo on my thigh. Nope, that's not coming up in casual conversation.

I started writing a day or two later, after coming up with a loose plot incorporating some of the ideas we hatched as kids. In a single night I wrote 25 pages of what would become AUD, and I sent it off to Joe with the message: Here bud, here's that story for you.

My intention was to write a chapter or two a week, send it to Joe, and we'd have fun with it. After Joe read the start of it, he wrote me back and asked, "What are we doing with this, because it's good, people will like it, and you should share it."

I fought him at first. Me? Share my writing? Fuck that. That would invite criticism and ridicule. He wouldn't take no for an answer, and he built a website, and we started to post the entries and such, and the world was introduced to Adrian Ring. Day one we had 23 visitors, and 444 hits. I'll never forget those numbers.

AUD exploded. Within days we had fifty regular readers a day, and within weeks a hundred. A month saw us reach a few hundred, and within six months we had thousands of daily readers, all chomping at the bit for me to post the next entry in Adrian's journal.

Now, it's published in book form, and is being translated into German by Voodoo Press. Audio books are in process. It's been read by over fifty thousand people, and book one, *Dark Recollections*, has a 4.81 average review on Amazon. The subsequent books in the series are even higher rated.

I've got shirts now, hats, stickers, and more. It's a thing.

Adrian is flawed. He begins the story arrogant, cocky, and sure he's the best person for the job. He's wrong, but he'll figure that out in time. He's also funny. And foul mouthed. But he loves his cat Otis, and reading with him, inside his head as he spills it all out in his journal you'll learn to love the big guy, whether he deserves it or not. Alongside his entries you'll find short stories inserted that expand the scope of the world of AUD, and fill in the blanks that Adrian couldn't know about. AUD is raw. It's spiritual in a way that's hard to describe. It's changed lives, and more than mine. It's fan base is rabid. I'm a lucky guy for having written it.

Here's a sampler of the start of *Dark Recollections*, the beginning of the eight book epic of Adrian's Undead Diary.

Enjoy.

September 21st

It's pretty fucking cold out tonight. The big ass plastic thermometer on the tree outside says its 35F out tonight. I'm glad I figured out where the emergency generator is here, otherwise I would be freezing my balls off now. Despite the fact that this place was kind of a bitch to clear out, I'm glad I did it. It's got everything I need to survive for a long time.

I don't even really know where to start. It's a Tuesday today. At least I know what day it is. Someone in the main office building was wise enough to buy their calendar early this year so it'll be easy for me to keep track of the days until the end of next year. After that I guess I'll have to use some of the graph paper and make my own calendar. That's being pretty optimistic though. The way the last few months have been I'll be goddamn lucky to make Christmas, let alone next Christmas.

I decided to start writing this mainly to keep track of my daily activities and to have a way to purge my nugget. Frankly I talk to myself way too goddamn much to be mentally healthy and I was always told that writing a journal helped. Sooo.. let's call this my journal. Thank God for spell check. I also realize that now is not the best time to be writing. I'm using up some of my gasoline to run the generator, which is basically a waste, and honestly having any lights on at night draws them in. Moths to a flame as the old saying goes. But I can't sleep and I've been meaning to do this for a long time now. Having the electricity back has set a fire under my ass to do this.

My name is Adrian Ring. I lived what I would now call as only a moderately successful life. I was happy, but I had pretty low standards. I had a girlfriend, I had a small condo downtown, I still have my cat (score!), and I have thus far avoided being eaten by the undead. Surprise! There's the twist in the story. I fucking love horror movies. Like seriously. I watched well over a thousand of them and always used to plot and plan should zombies ever rise from the dead and take over the world. Irony in all that is that when the shit hit the fan it happened so fast that any kind of plan would've been almost impossible to execute.

I was at work the night it started. I used to work third shift at a private school as a dorm supervisor. It was out of the way up in the hills outside of downtown, and only had about 100 students. Over 100k a year to attend. Very elite, very snooty, and basically the best job you could ask for. I had 9 hour shifts where I basically just made sure the kids didn't run away, and had their needs taken care of. Most nights I would do maybe an hour of work. I spent the rest of the time fucking around online looking at stupid videos and screwing around on the big ole f-book. God I wish I could update my status right now. Something really witty like "hasn't been eaten yet, so is pretty stoked." Or maybe something like, "wishes he grabbed more bullets when he raided the gun store in town." I dunno. Something cool.

Anyway, I was at work when it all hit. Working nights meant I was totally alone aside from the three other overnights and the sleeping kids, so when I checked the news websites and saw the few updates about "zombie hoaxes" I laughed. After a few hours more and more popped up on other websites, but I didn't take it too seriously. After all Halloween was coming up soon I figured it was some kind of stunt to promote a new movie or tv show. It wasn't until the morning when half the day shift people didn't show that I really realized something was up.

I went home as I normally do, and nothing seemed amiss. I called my girlfriend on the short drive home and we chatted. I asked her about it and she basically said she thought it was a hoax or some stunt. She was still half asleep though, so who knows what she really saw or heard on tv. Plus she was getting ready for work herself. She was gone by the time I got home, and I never saw her again. I think she was killed at work, or maybe on the drive home from work. I'll never know. The cities are far too dangerous for me to attempt to go to, and to be honest, as much as I loved her, it scares the shit out of me when I think of getting eaten alive. If you can read this babe, I love you.

I went to bed after watching a few minutes of the news and eating a banana. I can still remember the weird vibe on the good morning shows. Kinda tense, but sort of laughing it off. I can still remember the look on the dude's face as he reported it, kinda like he was waiting for an "april fools!" to pop up on his teleprompter. Never came I guess. So I went to bed.

I slept pretty good until about 3pm. I remember distinctly waking with a start, jarred awake. It took me a few minutes to piece together what actually woke me up, but the second gunshot kinda solved that riddle. It came from outside my window in the condo complex and I knew instantly something was very wrong.

My curtains are taped right to the window frames to block out the light, so I pulled on my gym shorts and hustled downstairs to look out the glass slider on the back side of the house. The action had ended by the time I got down there, but about thirty feet from where my place is I could clearly see a dead body laying in the parking lot. Have you ever seen someone take a shotgun blast to the head? Its horrible. There's no head left to speak of, first off, and secondly the body just empties the blood out of what's left of the head. More of a neck by that point really.

The body, a woman incidentally, was kind of laying towards my place, kinda downhill, and the blood was running into the mulch at the foot of the pine tree right behind my place. I've seen dead bodies before, I've been around violence plenty of times, but this was weird. It was in my neighborhood. You know, your sanctuary? I imagine the way I felt looking at her head-stump empty was a lot like watching your house burn down, or coming home to realize your house had been broken into. I felt violated. Anyway, I grabbed my sweatshirt, my cell phone, slipped my sandals on and sprinted out the back, dialing 911 as I went. I tripped over a root from the fucking pine tree and ate shit on the way, but I got there.

She was dead, of that there was no doubt. Her head was absolute demolished. She was wearing a garish flowery pattern shirt that looked a lot like the kind of shirts that a pediatric nurse would wear. She definitely had pants that looked a lot like those greenish scrub pants you see nurses wearing. I made my decision. Headless shotgun woman had been a nurse only a short time ago. At that point I realized my 911 call wasn't going through. Getting the all circuits' busy bullshit, which instantly set off my oh-shit radar. My groggy ass brain finally started to put two and two together. The zombie shenanigans from last night may not have been a hoax.

I don't own a gun. My girlfriend was kinda twitchy, and she had a little bit of a temper, and I really didn't want a firearm around that cocktail. It was far too foreseeable to see me getting shot because she thought I was a robber or something. So no guns. I did however own a few very high quality swords. Competently made and purchased at a few nerd festivals over the years. I really didn't want to grab a sword and just go driving around on the outside chance that this was just a random shooting, but I knew I had to get the fuck back inside one way or the other. If this was a random shooting, the random shooter was still pretty fucking nearby and I was not in the mood to get head-stumped myself.

So I ran inside. This time I did not eat shit on the root from the pine tree, and made it inside like an Olympic sprinter. I do remember being really pissed at myself because I left the slider open and my frigging cat Otis was sitting right on the fringe watching me the time. I didn't want him to get out, as he's an inside cat. He's a Maine Coon, so he's a beefy guy, but I woulda been pissed if he got hit by a car, or shot by a psycho with a twelve gauge. Seems like a reasonable concern considering the prior events, right? Whatever dude. I love my cat. He's my homeboy.

So by then I'd tried dialing 911 like 4 times. I had the

number for the police station already in my contacts so I called that line, and I got their automated response. The emergency choice just routed me to 911, and I was right back where I started. At that point I knew shit was bad. Can't be a coincidence. I hit the tv on and there it was, the EAS message. You know that irritating noise you hear when they're testing the emergency system? And very fucking rarely is there ever an emergency. I mean I guess in the midwest when they get tornadoes, or in the south when a hurricane is coming it's more relevant than here. All we ever get is shit like "emergency snowstorm warnings," or shit like road closures or accidents.

I'll never forget the message from that day:

State and local agencies are reporting widespread attacks on citizens across the region. Authorities are advising people to stay inside, lock their doors, bar their windows and only open doors for known friends and family who respond intelligently.

That was it. No mention of a virus, aliens attacking, zombies, vampires, or any such nonsense. I mean, I know now after having seen it a few hundred times we're dealing with zombies, but that message had no info at all. For the astute horror fan though, that's when I knew it was "on." You know, as in "it's on like Donkey Kong." I tried calling my girlfriend, both on her cell phone, and at her work extension, but no dice. I'm pretty fortunate in that I don't panic, like, ever. I've got years of experience dealing with violence, and I just don't lose my cool when the shit hits the fan. I'm the kind of dude you want making decisions in dangerous situations. Enough about me, I'm writing history now. More about me later when I have less to write about.

I knew she was dead. Or at least, damn close to it. None of the channels would work so I grabbed my laptop and fired it up. After connecting to my network I went to all the news websites and immediately found out I was right.

Picture after picture after cell phone video after news broadcast. All showing the zombies. Of course, no one had the fucking balls to call it like that. People were calling it everything but. Theories abounded everywhere I pointed the mouse. But I knew. You could see it. They were dead already, and didn't attack others until they'd passed on. I knew I needed to know a few things immediately about whatever it was that was doing this, so I got all scientific, and went to the CDC website.

They were on the ball, thankfully, and had the info as best as they could, already up. I needed to know a few things specifically:

• Transmission. How did it get transmitted? According to the CDC transmission occurred only via bite. Scratches did not seem to pass along the sickness/curse/virus/evil. Further, they had confirmed that the illness did not spread to non-human victims. Apparently a farm in Pennsylvania had all their cows eaten by the zombies and they stayed dead. (Of course later on I realized that this was somewhat wrong. You see by that point I don't think they had realized that anyone who died and didn't get their nugget wrecked immediately would get back up, seeking out flesh, being a general motherfucking nuisance to the living. But, I worked with what I knew at that point)

• Did they eat flesh? The CDC confirmed that yes, they did indeed eat the flesh of the living.

• Were the undead/sick/ill/terrorists that ate flesh more or less dangerous than a normal human being? Once again the CDC reported that the ill were slow, had diminished capacity for thought and reason, and were hostile to other human beings as well as animals. They were uncoordinated, couldn't move much faster than a clumsy trot at best, and showed no ability to communicate, or to make plans of any sort.

AT LEAST HE'S NOT ON FIRE

• Where did it all start? How close was I to "ground zero?" The CDC had no fucking clue. They said that there were about ten dozen simultaneous reports from all over the world. Plus or minus a few hours, which globally speaking is pretty fucking simultaneous. As best as I could figure, I was about a two hour drive from the closest outbreaks on the eastern seaboard.

• Could they be killed, and if so, how were they killed? According to the CDC (by now my most trusted source for news regarding the current and ongoing Zombie apocalypse) any significant damage done to the brain would drop them again. So Romero, dude you were totally spot-on. Fucking A brother.

So there it was. Despite the fact that even the CDC avoided calling it a "zombie outbreak" or the "apocalypse" I fucking knew. Well, at the very least, I wasn't about to risk it. I grabbed up my phone and tried to make a few more phone calls, but no joy. All circuits still busy. So, I formulated my plan.

Mom lived about a mile away, right near downtown, right near the schools, and I knew I would swing by her place to see if she was okay. I had a few friends who lived right around town too, and I wanted to check on them. More importantly though, was a long term survival plan. My condo was shitty in terms of a place to hole up, so I needed a place to go. I knew almost immediately I would come here, back to the school. It had everything.

I would get guns, some supplies, food, and then head to the school. Ride it out from there and see what happens. As you can tell, I made it here in one piece. But that doesn't tell the whole story. Unfortunately my guilt over wasting this gas has finally reached its boiling point. Plus I'm getting really fucking tired and I need to lock the upstairs down so I can sleep soundly.

I think for my next entry I'll talk about the trip to get here. And what I found when I did.

Until next time Mr. Journal.

-Adrian

September 27th

Hi Mr. Journal. I think it's all starting to get to me. I did not have a very good week here at all. Nothing bad happened, which is awesome really, but I think spilling my guts last Tuesday opened up some fucking epic wounds I had really forgotten about.

I'm sitting here with tears welling up in my eyes as I think about the fact that I did not go and at least try and find Cass. Cassie. Just typing her name is hard for me to do right now. I sat here looking at this blank white sheet of pixilated paper for almost an hour just trying to think of something to write about but I couldn't. All I could think about was the fact that my awesome goddamn plan that day didn't include at least trying to rescue the woman I should've married.

I mean, I'm alive, and that's good, but it all seems pretty fucking pointless without her here. Like, why do I even bother to make myself dinner when she's not here to tell me how bad my cooking is? We were together for so long and I just don't know why I didn't ask her to marry me sooner. Fear of commitment? Wedding was too expensive? Was I afraid her parents would say no? Shit I don't know. And it kills me I never will know. My mouth is bone dry right now. I can't even swallow.

I've sat in bed, snuggled up with Otis and just laid there thinking about this. I've been so busy getting this place safe from the zombies that I haven't had time to really think about it until now. She has to be dead, right? She was never the "survivor" type. She lost her goddamn mind when there was a spider in the house, I can't envision her keeping her shit together when people are dying all around her, then sitting up and attacking her too. My most frequent delusion about her death is that she died in a car accident trying to get out of the city. You know, she would've taken the stairs to get out of the building, ran to her car, dodging the undead's awkward lunges. I can see her starting her little car, backing out into the street, and then getting creamed at an intersection by some fucking asshole in a giant SUV trying to do the same thing as her. In my guilt filled vision she not only is killed instantly, but is either decapitated, or is so mangled that she can't get back up as the undead.

I think thinking of it that way makes me feel like it's better that way. At least if she died that way she isn't hurting anyone else, and at least that way I will never have to worry about seeing her disintegrating body shambling towards me someday. Man I hope that never happens. I don't think I could take seeing that. Seeing her beautiful face all ashen and bloody, teeth bared, slowly clawing at the air as she comes toward me.

Just typing that makes my fucking skin crawl.

There's this enormous part of me that says I should go get a truck from the maintenance barn and make my way to her work. For closure. I know I won't find her, at least, I know I won't find her alive. I think if I did find her car smashed to shit in an intersection I might feel better about myself. About my decision that day. You know at least I could say that I was right about not going to try and find her. She was probably already dead by the time I even knew what was going on that day. There was no chance that I could've saved her.

Then the little prick inside me says; "Adrian, but what if you find her dead, walking along the road, slowly making her way home, slowly making her way back to you?" And my ambition to go get closure just dries right the fuck up. I think that little prick, that little voice inside me is my cowardice. I never thought of myself as a coward. Really. I've waded into some pretty dangerous shit in my 34 years on this planet, and not once did I give it a second thought.

Why the fuck did I give up on her so easily that day?

Fuck you Mr. Journal.

-Adrian

September 28th

Mr. Journal I'm profoundly sorry for my outburst at the end of the last journal. Good sentence right there. I think a few of my English teachers just rolled over in their graves. Well actually a few of my English teachers probably just burped up the entrails of a few of my math teachers, but you get the idea. Sorry surviving English teachers, that was pretty tasteless.

Pun not intended.

I feel better about myself today. I think yesterday's journal entry was cathartic for me. Finally admitting out loud that I failed myself and Cass that day has relieved me of some guilt. I actually slept pretty good last night for the first time since my first journal entry. I've been restless for a long time, and it was really rejuvenating to get a full 8 hours of sleep. Otis can sense my troubles too, and it has had him on edge. He's been largely avoiding me for a few days now, and finally this morning he actually came up to me as I woke up and looked for some attention. Apparently he can figure out when I'm emotionally capable of giving him some affection. I am so thankful he's still around.

After I gave him his love this morning I had a bit of a startle. The campus here is pretty fucking out of the way. We're at the end of a country dead end road in a small town, miles from anything even remotely looking like civilization.

AT LEAST HE'S NOT ON FIRE

There are maybe fifteen houses along the five miles heading up the hills to get here. Our campus is surrounded by water. There is a lake all along one side of the property, and the lake has a river draining down the hill we're on that skirts the other side of the property. Shit, you need to cross a bridge to get here. It's as close as you can get to an island without needing a boat. Hence part of its allure as a last ditch place to hold up. I parked two of the transport vans we used to use to get the kids around use on the far side of the bridge and there's no way anything can get across. Someone could climb across the top, but the zombies are far too stupid to put that plan together. Living people would need to get out and cross on foot if they were coming to visit.

I hate using my guns now. A: It's a waste of ammunition, B: we have an archery range here, and arrows are reusable if I do it right, and C: guns are loud, and could theoretically draw unwanted attention. Anyway, when I went out to check the campus for dead folk, lo and behold there were two zombies shuffling and milling about on the far side of the vans. I don't think they knew I was here, but honestly, I didn't ask them. It took me three arrows to hit both of them in the head and re-kill them, so to speak. My first shot just thunked right into the dry, empty eye socket of the first zombie. He dropped like a bag of wet laundry. My second shot sailed pretty wide right, not sure why, it felt good when I let it go. But, third time's the charm, and I hit the other zombie squarely in his brainpan. I sat still for a bit, waiting to see if there were any other undead dudes on the other side of the bridge, and after a bit, I crossed carefully and retrieved all three arrows. All three were fine for use again.

I really didn't want to leave those bodies there, so I got my rubber gloves, my shitty overalls, and got the four wheeler with the little trailer on it, moved the vans, and drove the two corpses to the far back side of the campus, out where the faculty residences are. Or used to be. Not sure what the proper tense is on that. I mean technically, the residences are still there, but the faculty that used to live in them is long since gone. I guess it doesn't matter. Both of the bodies were heavy as hell, and smelled fucking awful. Not the sick, rotting putrid flesh smell, more of a rotting fecal matter and kelp odor. I know, charming.

Anyhoo… moved the vans back, chilled out for a bit to make sure everything was quiet, and I hit the campus cafeteria and snagged some canned stuff to eat for the day. I'm finally getting accustomed to moving about without the constant fear of being attacked around every corner. At first, right after all the shit started, I moved through life in a slow and smooth combat walk, gun at the ready. Every single door was breached like I was either a super secret sneaky spy, or like I was kicking in a door in a slum in Baghdad, looking for wahabi.

It's only been the last few days that I've felt safe enough to basically just live life like "normal." Lol. Normal. What the fuck is that now? Normal is not being pretty okay with watching a dead human being gnawing away at the flesh of a slowly dying person. Normal is not reasoning with yourself that everything in that situation is okay, because the zombie is busy eating that person, and will thus not attack you for some time, ergo, you are "safe." How fucked up is that?

So I'm feeling pretty good right now. I have some warmed up canned corned beef hash, a couple slices of canned brown bread, and some hot instant coffee. I'm feeling a little better about my utter scumbaggery re: leaving the love of my life to die a bitter, lonely death, and I actually feel like dropping more into this journal. Sound okay to you Mr. Journal?

I thought you'd like the attention. Soon as I get Otis off the screen of the laptop, I'll tell you a story.

There we go. I'm sure he'll be back up in my lap shortly anyway. I'll get done what I can in the meantime.

Where was I? So I had formulated a plan to get to what I felt was relative safety. Food, supplies, guns, check on friends and family, and get here to the school. Not necessarily in that order. I live about 2 miles from the local gun store. I could see and hear cars still driving by on main street outside the complex so I knew it wasn't total devastation. Probably panicked, probably fucked up a lot, but probably still, you know, held together.

After I got dressed, I grabbed a mess of shit and loaded my car. A suitcase and a duffel bag of clothes were first. I grabbed my two best swords, and strapped my dad's old hunting knife to my belt. It's a badass knife my uncle made a long time ago out of a piece of heavy duty file. It looks like something straight out of horror movie. I use an old K-Bar sheathe for it for when I go hiking, so it looks even more badass. Like how badass I look is going to help when I am getting mauled by the undead, right? Very feminine of me to think about how I look at a time like that. Cass always said I was sensitive.

I snagged an old plastic milk crate and loaded all the food in the kitchen that would last into it. Everything canned, everything frozen, anything bottled. I filled every water bottle we had, and dumped out the milk jugs, and filled those with water too. No idea how long running water would be available, and I wanted as much as possible. I grabbed Cass' sewing kit, my dad's old fishing rod and tackle box, our first aid kit, and my toolbox. I grabbed a few other odds and ends like boots and shoes, miscellaneous items that might come handy, books, some hobby oriented shit, and then I got Otis into his travel cage thingy. He fucking despises that thing with a passion. Some of worst scars have come from him fighting me when I try and get him in there. That day though, he was pretty good.

I remember vividly one of my last memories of my condo that day was seeing that nurse's body in the parking lot again. Her blood wasn't anywhere near as red on the pavement anymore. It had already started to turn a muddy, rusty brown color, which is normal. Blood is bright red, especially when it's arterial blood, which is what she had been squirting all over the place when I first saw her. I can remember still that seeing her body the second time around didn't weird me out at all. I think I can attribute that to two things; first, my natural sense of calm when the shit hits the fan, and second, I knew that the nurse was probably undead when she was shot. It kind of made me feel good to know that someone had the presence of mind to drop her quickly. Of course I also wonder today that maybe someone just blew her head off and was going to use the whole zombie thing as an excuse. The more I think about it, the more plausible some variation of that idea seems right. After all, when you kill a zombie, they don't really bleed, they just kinda… ooze. She was totally squirting. Sounds totally dirty. Maybe she had just been bitten, was still alive, and then she got shot? Who knows.

My last memory from my place was seeing her body in the parking lot. I loaded Otis in the car, double checked that I had everything I would need, and we were off to Moore's Sporting Goods. Moore's was a scene straight out of an end of the world movie. There was a cop in the parking lot providing barely adequate security as like 30 cars filled with people stormed in and out of the shop, buying everything in sight. I remember being suddenly doubtful of me being able to get anything at all there, but I was there, and I had to go in.

I know all the cops in town on a first name basis, or at least by face, and the cop in the parking lot was one I've known for years. Officer McGreevy. Big dude, bigger than me, and that's saying something. Bald as shit though, which is something I'm not. He was struggling trying to talk to a few panicked older people and we exchanged glances. I knew just from the look on his face shit was bad all over. He had that no nonsense, shit was bad look on his face. You know the one.

There was almost a line to get into the shop. Luckily Moore's had extra people behind their counter, so they were ringing people up pretty quickly. I noticed a few big hastily scribbled signs taped up in conspicuous places around the shop, each said the same thing;

There is a one rifle, one handgun, and one shotgun limit per customer. Thank you, Moore's.

Good enough. If you couldn't figure out how to get through this with all that, you were fucked anyway I think. I waited patiently in the three deep crowd at the counter until one of the clerks finally motioned for me to come up. I can remember his nametag was crooked, like the little safety pin had come undone in the back. His name was Phil. Phil was overweight like I was, had salt and pepper hair, and the look of a person who had had fucking enough. I made my decision to keep it professional.

I calmly requested to Phil that I was interested in a Glock handgun, preferably a 9mm or .40 caliber, a pump or semi auto shotgun, preferably 12 or 16 gauge, and a semi-automatic .22 caliber rifle, one preferably with a magazine. He told me they were flat out of Glocks entirely, but they did have a few Sig 9mm's left. I told him that was fine, and he got the rest of my order.

Now I'm not saying the fine folks of Moore's made a poor decision that day, or that our legal system failed our nation, but there was NO background check performed on anyone while I was there. Now I have a clean record, but some of the folks there were Shady as hell. Capital S added for extra emphasis on Shady.

Phil was nice enough to sell me 2,000 rounds of the .22 cal ammo, 200 rounds of 9mm, and 48 12 gauge double ought shells. He told me he was giving me the "hook up" and even sold me two spare magazines (that's a clip, for the uninformed) for both the rifle and the pistol. Those would be a big deal as you'll see in later entries. I also got a few extra things of gun oil, a fresh gun cleaning kit, as well as a holster and a hunting vest to wear for the shotgun shells and supplies.

The line had died down pretty dramatically while Phil

waited on me, and he and I chatted a bit. The folks here were in tight with the cops and they had a better local feel for what was up. Apparently there were no zombies from here, yet. The few zombies seen nearby were people who had come in from out of state already bitten, or already sick somehow. Of course, those few folks had bitten some other folks, and it was slowly spreading. The cops were doing a great job of containing shit from the sound of it, but even after hearing that, I wasn't fucking around. I had Phil charge it all on my credit card, and walked out more or less armed to the teeth.

Officer McGreevy was currently unimpeded by panicked customers when I walked out, so I waved hello, and he tiredly waved back. I loaded up my weapons, illegally, right in front of him in the parking lot, and we exchanged one last wave.

As I drove away down the road, I heard a few gunshots from behind me, back down where the shop was. I stomped the brakes, threw it in reverse, and backed down the road into the parking lot. A new car with out of state plates was in the lot, and McGreevy had his weapon drawn on the vehicle. One of the Moore's employees (not our intrepid hero clerk Phil) was in the doorway, handgun drawn as well. From inside my car I could see that the driver of the out of state sedan was face down on the ground, bleeding a circle out underneath him. The passenger of the car was a little boy, maybe 14 years old, brown hair, screaming bloody murder. McGreevy's pistol shot once more, caving in the back of the dude's head, splattering shit everywhere on the fender of the car. I noticed then that the guy had a huge red mark on the sleeve of his dress shirt. Looked an awful lot like a big fucking bite mark.

My guess was he looked sick, McGreevy saw the bite mark, and made a quick decision. I could see clearly from his face the cop was not cool with what had just happened. I could also see the Moore's guys coming out, practically celebrating that they had "gotten one." McGreevy looked up at me in my car, sighed once, and nodded really slightly. The kid was still screaming.

I never saw any of them again.

-Adrian

October 4th

Hello again Mr. Journal. You know all this week I was wondering to myself why I sort of randomly decided that you were Mr. Journal, as opposed to Ms. Journal, or Mrs. Journal, or even Miss journal. Maybe I am subconsciously only comfortable spilling my guts to an artificial male? Dunno. Maybe at a later date I'll decide to spill my guts to a new target audience and change it (you)to Miss Journal. Maybe Miss Journal will want my shit, and I'll get laid again. Guess I should make my stories good then eh? Another thought occurs to me though; if I change Mr. Journal to Miss Journal, and I'm hoping Miss Journal wants my shit does that mean I'm into trannies? Now there's a Zen train of thought for you.

It's been a pretty good week since my last entry. Not much of anything has happened here on campus. I spent the majority of my time working in the vocational building in the woodshop. We had a shit-ton of lumber stored there and I was working on making myself some barricades. The dorms here aren't like you'd imagine for a normal boarding school. They aren't like Hogwart's, and they aren't like apartment buildings. We have five dorm buildings all broken up by age groups and grades. Each building is more or less like a giant house. Three of the dormitories are two floors, one is three floors, and one is just one floor. Stylistically they are all pretty similar to houses, but they're beefed up and industrialized.

Each dorm's exterior doors are all fire doors with heavy

duty locks. That means they are steel, lock when they close, and are set in heavy duty frames. Perfect for fending off zombie attacks basically. Now each dorm has certain perks going for it. Hall A is good because it's dead center in campus. Windows in the dorm face in all directions, and it's got a great view of the bridge that people (or the undead) would cross to get here. Hall A is shitty because the first floor is very low to the ground. Its windows would be easy to break, and there are a lot of windows for the breaking. The second floor is good because the two stairwells are separate from the first floor, both are behind fire doors, and they're on separate ends of the building. Plus the second floor has a little balcony off the staff apartment that used to belong to Mr. Trendwell, the physics teacher.

Hall E is about 200 feet down the sidewalk from A. Both Hall E and Hall A are near the river that skirts campus, which is nice when you open a window. You can hear the babbling of the water, and it's relaxing. Hall E has a lot of things going for it. It's kind of on the edge of a hill, and there are no windows on ground level. The bottom of the windows start at about five feet above ground level, so breaking a window would be difficult for a zombie. I've already got those windows barricaded with 2x4's and plywood, so that's covered. I was clever and only blocked off the bottom two thirds of the windows so I could still see out the window, or shoot out them if necessary. Other benefits of Hall E are as follows: Full kitchen, three floors, two living rooms, standard issue double fire doors at both entrances, and 18 bedrooms. Hall E seemingly had the least drawbacks, so that's where I'm set up now.

I'll tell more about the campus and the other buildings here later. Just about every building here has some kind of fucked up story to tell about it, and I don't want to miss any of the juicy details. Gotta impress Miss Journal for when she shows up, right?

The barricades I worked on this week were for some of the buildings that are low to the ground here. Specifically I

AT LEAST HE'S NOT ON FIRE

really want to get the deck on the end of Hall E more secure. It's on the edge of the building that's overhanging the hill, so it's about 8 feet off the ground, but I really want to shore up the railings in the event I'm swamped and trapped here. So that was my project this week. I had enough lumber, skill and ambition to get that project done. Huzzah me. The whole time I was working in the shop I kept my shotgun handy, and didn't use any of the power tools. Noise is bad, and plus there's no sense in wasting my gas. My supply is obviously limited, and it's not like I've got more important shit to do. Handsaws for the win.

I think I should probably fill in more details about my trip here though. There's still so much story left just from the day the world fell apart. I'll be talking about it in journal entries until Thanksgiving more than likely.

So I think I said earlier that things happened so fast a plan was kind of impossible. Everything according to my plan had gone pretty much perfectly up until the shooting at Moore's. And really, that incident didn't change my plan at all. That was the first really fucked up thing I was sort of involved in that day, so I kind of look at that as the tipping point where things started to seriously come undone for me.

So I left the gun shop and started to update my plan. I now had guns and ammo. The most important and useful things from my house were in my trunk and backseat, so all I needed to do was to check on my friends, and stock up on food. Non-perishable stuff of course. As I got off the side street Moore's is on I saw the local agriculture store and it suddenly dawned on me I might need to grow food. I also noticed that the parking lot was almost empty so I made my first detour. Everyone in the store was huddled at the counter listening to the radio, and the news streaming out of it from NPR. I didn't want to waste any time, as it was already starting to get late, so I just went straight to the seed display. I literally grabbed one little pouch of everything they had, and snagged one of those garden weasel dealies. I knew the grounds keeping equipment at the school would probably have whatever else I needed. I remember it took me asking about ten times before the chick running the register even realized I was waiting to pay. She rang me up totally wrong, and only charged me like 15 bucks for everything. I had enough cash, so I paid, took my bag and garden aero-ater thingamabob, and walked out totally unnoticed.

All that shit went into the backseat and I was off again. When I was about to pull out of the parking lot one of the town ambulances flew by, headed down the road Moore's was on. I assumed they were headed to deal with the shooting. Another one of our town's finest was right on the ambulance's ass as well. That was actually the last time I saw a cop. Weird now to think that it's been months since I've seen a cop. Weird now to think that the dead come alive and feast on the flesh of the living too. Lols and whatnot.

Sooo.... Our local chain grocery store is on the other side of downtown, about 3 miles or so from where I was. I knew it'd be a madhouse, but I really needed food. I drove just under the speed limit mostly because I wanted to scan the surroundings for weirdness. Oddly enough, I saw little. There were a lot of people packing their cars, and I saw a lot of dads and son out in the yard hammering nails into sheets of plywood covering windows. I saw one desperate dude hammering up a door over a window and had to laugh. I wonder still how many of those folks are still holed up in their houses. I haven't done any tests, but I imagine a sheet of plywood wouldn't last long against a bunch of the undead hitting it over and over. Granted, they are weaker than a person, but they don't fucking get tired. The only "break" they take is to gnaw your flesh off your bones. Otherwise, they just keep at it, whatever it is they're doing.

Anyway, downtown was pretty tame. The power was still on, and I ran the red light cautiously in the center of town. There was no traffic, and I wanted to get to the store to get food before it was literally gobbled up. The final two miles to the store was more or less uneventful. I got passed on the road twice by jackasses driving giant pickup trucks. One of them flipped me off as he passed me on a solid yellow and I just had to laugh. World is ending and this guy is such a dink that he has give me the finger for not doing 60 in a 30. Some people are just assholes. I hope he got eaten by another asshole. The second guy who passed me was much nicer though. No middle finger.

The grocery store was mobbed, as I thought it would be. I parked on the edge of the parking lot and locked up the car. I slipped on my hunting vest, loaded it up with the shells Phil hooked me up with, and slung the shotgun over my shoulder. It was that moment that realized I needed to shorten the barrel and stock on the shotgun somehow. It was a little long and would be difficult to use in a building. I made a mental note to myself on that for later. I could clearly see other folks leaving the store carrying hunting rifles, so I wasn't too worried about the "social norm" of carrying a 12 gauge. I did get the opportunity to watch some woman in a minivan fucking cream a dude walking in the parking lot though. She must've not seen him, cuz she just plowed through his ass and just drove on. The ass end of the minivan hopped up like it was on springs when she drove over him. A bunch of folks rushed over to help him right after, so I didn't feel obligated to. I snagged a cart out of the corral and just like Johnny Shopper, I went in the automated door, and straight into retail hell.

You ever been grocery shopping the week of Thanksgiving? Or right before Christmas, when all the soccer moms lose their fucking mind and fight over boxes of shitty stuffing mix and cranberry relish? Well imagine that, and then add an "end of the world" flavor to it. That'll get you in the ballpark for the mood everyone had in the store that afternoon. I think it was about 5 or 5:30 at that point. Just starting to get dark-ish, and I can remember the temp getting low as the sun was setting.

Anyway, the lines were packed, and people were literally running their carts around the store, up and down the aisles like with reckless abandon. There were kids hollering at the top of their lungs as their moms and dads shopped literally like there was no tomorrow. I can't even imagine what a six year old would make of the situation. PTSD without a doubt for our children now. If there are any children left. Like all grocery stores, the majority of the canned goods are in the center of the store. Most of the folks were in those two aisles, so I decided to start on the fringe, and get other shit first. By the time I was done I had grabbed an entire shopping cart of food and supplies. Felt like I was pushing a pallet of bricks. I hit the pharmacy area hardcore and loaded up on bandages, ibuprofen, cold remedies, vitamins, melatonin, bacitracin, etc. You name it, I grabbed it. I wasn't about to worry about running out of that stuff.

For those of you who are curious, yes, I did grab several boxes of yellow, crème filled snack cakes. I didn't want to risk wanting one and having to come back to get them. So I snagged a mess of frozen veggies and shit like that, and I eventually intimidated my way into the canned goods aisles. Six foot one with scary tattoos is > a soccer mom. I knew the school kept a lot of canned shit on hand, so I made sure to grab the stuff I knew they would likely have little or none of. Boyardee stuff obviously, and I grabbed a lot of tuna pouches, canned veggies and that righteously yummy canned brown bread you eat with beans. I also got the beans to go with it. Sneaky motherfucker that I am I slipped behind the deli counter when the clerks weren't looking and grabbed a few whole, still sealed slabs of meat. One each of turkey, ham and bologna.

Sooooo... my shamefulness comes back. The deli is kinda near the exit and it took about two seconds of deliberation before I decided I was going to walk the fuck out without paying. What were they going to do anyway? Every employee had either left already, or was gooch-deep in customers. The only shitty problem was that my groceries would not be bagged. Not a real problem. I'll deal with that.

Out the door I went, snagging two bunches of bananas

on the way. Outside things had gotten much fucking worse. Our grocery store patron who had been creamed by the soccer mom in her minivan was not doing well at all. Actually he had died, and someone had thrown a heavy duty blanket over him. One of those gray, industrial blankets people steal out of the back of moving trucks. I gave the crowd around his body a wide berth and made it about fifty more feet before I heard them start screaming. I stopped dead in my tracks, turned around, and watched the crowd scatter like dandelion fluff in the wind. I have never seen such fat people move with such vigor before. One lady with a mega-fupa was literally tearing up pavement as she ran. I still laugh today thinking of her jiggling rolls as she nearly ate shit getting into her far too small compact car. It might've been the springs, but I swear to this day I heard her car cry out in pain when she got in it.

Anyway, our poor accident victim had sat back up. From my angle at the time he was kind of facing away from me, and he still had the blanket covering his front side. He was blind basically with the blanket over his face. Morbid curiosity found me unslinging the shotgun, and approaching the dude. I racked up a round in the chamber and slowly circled him at about ten feet. You could just tell from his body language that he was fucked up. Plus he was making this rattling noise with his quasi-breathing that was just not normal. Well that's not entirely true. Ever give someone CPR? Frequently when you're giving real CPR air gets down into the stomach. When the air escapes it sometimes does this burpish-gurgle deal that's kind of unsettling. It's the death-rattle you read about. This dude was doing it, and he was moving around at the same time. Didn't make sense. I knew what it really meant though.

Just about when I got to his 10 o'clock the blanket slipped off his face, and I saw my first zombie. He was lit the fuck up. That accident had made him royally fucking nasty, and add to that all his color had drained away. His skin was this ashen white with a blue tinge. Dried blood crusted the edge of his mouth. He tried to stand up to come at me but both his legs were shattered. He kinda half fell over in my direction and face planted on the pavement. I remember laughing nervously when he started crawling at me because I saw his face had left a bloody wet mark where it had hit down.

His eyes had totally glazed over and were almost whitish-grey. He wasn't moaning like they do in the movies either. It makes a lot of sense now that I've seen so many real zombies. Moaning requires breathing, and these things do not breathe. Once he had finished his charming death-rattle, he was silent. That's actually one of the things that keeps me up at night. If you don't hear the shuffling of their feet, see them coming, or smell them coming, they are almost entirely silent.

After I made the mental decision that this man was indeed a newly minted zombie I took a deep breath, drew a bead on his face, closed my eyes, and pulled the trigger. The Mossberg bucked hard, and I felt something hit the front of my pants. I opened my eyes and saw that his face was totally annihilated, and some of the splash had hit me in the legs. I panicked for a second, wondering if this shit was contagious. I took another deep breath and chilled myself out. Couldn't worry too much about it right then. I racked up another shell in the shotgun, noticed the startling amount of people looking at me with shocked expressions, and walked back to my cart. You know there were at least ten guys in the parking lot at that moment with a gun just like me. Why didn't they do anything? Was I the only one with balls? I suspect I have just watched too many horror movies.

The crowds parted like I was mother-fucking Moses and they were the Red Sea. I'm a big dude, and frequently people see me and my tattoos and I get a wide berth anyway, but this was an adult-strength wide berth. 20 feet solid. That kinda felt good. I was getting a hardcore adrenaline rush the whole time and I'm not gonna lie, it felt kind of good.

I scooped my groceries into the trunk of my car, topping it off. I grabbed the box of shotgun shells from the passenger

AT LEAST HE'S NOT ON FIRE

seat of my car, loaded a replacement shell in for the one I just shot, and got in the car.
 Next stop: Friends and family.

 See you soon Mr. Journal.

 -Adrian

Hell Hole

I wrote Hell Hole as a submission to military horror anthology in early 2013. To be frank, I waited way too long to get started on it, and put in half the effort in half the time I should've. I wasn't surprised in the least that it was rejected by the publisher, and in a way, I was relieved. The publisher gave me honest criticism of the piece too, which I'm still thankful for. It really does help to be told what you're doing wrong.

This verson of Hell Hole saw significantly more editing and writing time. I've added over a thousand words to make it cleaner, and a little scarier, and I think now it would've had a chance to make the cut into that anthology. It's not my favorite piece by a long shot, but I'm happy to share it with you here so it at least sees the light of day somehow.

Enjoy.

Everything changed when that hole was found in the ground. At first people thought the world would end when nuclear missiles were shot across the big blue sky by the Russians, or the Americans. Didn't matter who shot first really. Han or Greedo, everyone would pay the price. Then they thought it would all come crashing down when the terrorists launched some kind of biological weapons attack. For a little while people thought the world would implode due to political strife, and economic failure, but in the end it all came down to a goddamn hole in the ground.

At first the media and the scientists tried to keep all the names straight, right next to all the ugly details, but that was abandoned when the cities started to collapse into the earth below. There's just too much to do when skyscrapers are getting tipped over. Warrant Officer 2 Anton Michaels was there when that first hole was found. He saw what came from the bottom. What churned underneath.

It happened about ten years ago, but no one gave a shit about calendars anymore. Well, the military did, and it seemed like everyone was either in the military, or working for the military now, so maybe people did give a shit about calendars.

Anton was a fresh Special Forces 18B at the time, straight from the Upper Peninsula of Michigan, his M4A1 in hand and attached to the 1st Special Forces Group. They were on an in-country training operation working with native Indonesian forces. With the Al-Qaeda activity in the island nation at an all time high, his group had been deployed for half a year every year for a very long time. Building the locals up to take down their internal threat was a high priority. Anton was overwhelmed by the heat and crushing humidity (it wasn't like this on the Peninsula), but seeing the deep jungle and bright blue ocean of the pacific islands was a true treat he relished. So what if he had bugs biting his balls, and more skin that was rash than not? He'd heal. He always did.

That time they were out with Kopassus, the Indonesian Special Forces group with the shady past. To help heal some wounds to the trust between the training units, the leader of the Kopassus unit offered to take the Green Berets to a nearly lost temple deep in the jungle. It was a once in a lifetime opportunity, and the unit couldn't say no. There were too many political ramifications of offending the host country, and that's not what Green Berets did.

"Candi, Candi!" the Indonesian military men said, pointing through the impenetrable jungle. Candi was their word for temple.

"Temple? Yeah?" Anton had asked.

"Temple, yes. Candi! Big Candi!" the young soldier said

AT LEAST HE'S NOT ON FIRE

back to Anton. The little Indonesian man couldn't have been more than twenty, but you could never really know how old they were. It seemed like they just got smaller as they aged, not wrinklier. He imagined a nation of tiny Indonesians running underfoot.

The Candi was small by Anton's judgment. They'd just visited the massive complex of Borobudur on the island of Java, and that was something. This little temple was no bigger than a two story house from the UP, but damn it did look old. Anton and his unit, led by their veteran team Captain followed the tiny Kopassus men down a hill into a depression between several hills in the rainforest. The leaf cover above was near total; the temple was only lit by tiny rays of sunlight that pierced holes in the leaves above like javelins sent from God. It was a surreal scene for Anton long before the hole became a part of the story.

The Kopassus men showed the Green Berets around the ancient temple, chattering in their language faster than the Americans could keep up, happy and excited to be sharing something so old and so important from their past. The Americans were delighted as well, sharing relieved expressions and groans of sore muscles. The temple meant time to sit and rest.

"Quite the place huh?" Sergeant Giancola asked as the two Green Berets took up security at the top of one of the small hills that formed the depression. The jungle here was empty of human threats, but they followed protocol anyway. Repetition in times of safety was important for building good habits in times of strife.

"Yeah. Reminds me of a museum I never go to back at home," Anton had said back. The two men chuckled, and went back to comfortable silence.

Ten minutes later one of the other men in the team came up the hill and tapped Anton on the shoulder. He was a hulking brute of a man with rippling muscles and a neck almost as wide as his shoulders. The guys on the team called him The Thing. "Go check the place out, I'll cover this. It's creepy as fuck. Really weird etchings in the stone. Gargoyles and shit."

Anton had nodded, thanked The Thing, and trotted down the hill to do as he was told. As soon as he entered, he knew the Sergeant was right; the temple *was* as creepy as fuck. On all four corners of the two story, cone shaped building were carvings and faded paintings of creatures that had to have been dreamt of. Worms with teeth the size of a man's hand sprouted from the earth and ate tiny figures of men who were running away, wild and fearful. Frescos and carvings depicted winged beasts sweeping down from cloud filled skies riding bolts of lightning that split rocks and sundered men and women alike. It was a vengeful scene, filled with wrath and ruin. It was a prophecy, but no one in the temple that day knew that yet.

"This ain't no Hindu temple," the team's Warrant Officer said with a strong Alabama accent. Anton wondered if he would even know what a real Hindu temple looked like. The WO answered the question immediately, "I've seen lots of Hindu temples in my time, and this ain't one, not by a long shot. This is like, satanic shit. Lovecraft shit. Ex-wife shit."

The Americans laughed. The tiny Indonesians had no idea what he was talking about but laughed along with them. Once the laughter faded, the local soldiers tried to explain the temple to the two soldiers who spoke their language decently. One of the Green Berets tried to translate. It was hard to keep up with the little brown soldier's rattling.

"Guy says that a long time ago, there was a deep hole where this temple is. Underneath where we are standing. Says it went down to uh, um, Hell or something. Caverns below maybe. Says all the local warriors rose up and defeated these creatures that came out of the hole in a war that lasted almost two years. He's saying that there were flying monsters, and big worm, or snake things. He said those were the real problem. They would um, eat the earth right out from under you. Swallow you whole."

"Bullshit. They're pranking us," another soldier said with

a grin. Soldiers appreciated a good joke at each other's expense. Sometimes it was the only way to smile in such a grim line of work.

The Captain of the A-Team shrugged. "Maybe so boys, but this place had some bad juju. I can feel it in my bones."

The interpreting soldier picked up the story as the local man continued. "Says the hole to 'Hell' was finally capped by this temple. Blessed by the local priests and all that jazz. Says that if the temple is ever destroyed, the things underneath it will come back, this time worse."

One of the other soldiers had dug out his entrenching tool and was digging at the corner of the temple where the earth rose up to meet it. He was bound and determined to find the hole the building sat on.

"Andrew cut the shit. This place is sacred," the Captain said quietly before the Kopassus men saw what he was doing. The Sergeant with the digging tool stopped and stood immediately, a sheepish grin on his face. "I'm going inside. Is that okay with these guys?"

The interpreting Green Beret asked them, and after some consultation, the Indonesians felt it was okay. The Captain thanked them, and ducked his head low and headed into the stone arched entryway. It was clearly made for much shorter people than the American. It was only a minute before he started yelling for his men. "Holy shit guys, Carl, Anton, get in here!"

The WO and Anton rushed into the breach, weapons up with safeties off as the local soldiers all hid a laugh on their faces. Anton was sure it was nothing, a prank like his buddy had said, but all that changed when he saw the look of terror on his Captain's face. The experienced warrior was backed into the stone outer wall of the cramped temple's single inner room, and his eyes were locked on the floor of the building. Anton looked as the Warrant Officer went to the Captain.

The center room of the temple was square, the same as the outside. The ceiling reached high into the upper levels of the odd, tiered cone roof, creating a room that was tall, yet oppressive. It felt like the weight of the world was crushing down from above. The floor of the room descended down multiple steep steps to a flat surface that was covered in human remains. Skeletons of men, women and children were piled nearly ten feet high, filling the sunken in floor and rising several feet higher than the floor the men stood on. The air was thick with dust, and hot, hard to breathe.

Perched atop the pile of bones at the center of the room was a creature that defied logic and science. It was humanoid, with arms long and sinuous at the shoulder. Its legs were bent backwards, like a goat's or a wolf's, and erupting from its back was a pair of wings that extended out nearly the width of the entire room. All its skin was black as pitch, and its eyes were crimson flecked with bright, alien orange. But all its humanity was lost in its mouth. Fanged like a lamprey's, and hinged like a snake's, the jaw flexed up and down hungrily at the Americans. Anton's primitive brain somehow let him realize that on some of the bodies underfoot the creature were uniforms. Australian uniforms. The Aussies trained with these people.

Anton didn't wait for orders to fire. Fuck the cultural exchange. He shouldered his weapon and squeezed the trigger as he'd been trained a hundred times over, and sent three high velocity rounds straight into the upper torso of the creature. His bullets struck true, but did nothing. They impacted the creature and rocked it backwards, but did no more damage than if he'd pushed the *thing* hard with his finger. Anton's heart dropped to his boots.

Gunfire erupted outside like an echo from Anton's burst. The first barrage was clearly not from the American M4s. It came from the Indonesian weaponry. The second barrage, only a second later, was easily identified as American. It was return fire. Anton's blood curdled when he heard the throaty roar of The Thing's scream.

"They're shooting on us! Return-" The Thing went silent. Anton knew he'd been shot, or was dead, but he had a more significant problem inside the temple as the creature leapt from the bone pile, soaring the twenty feet of distance on its infernal wings. It landed far too close to the soldiers and triggered a gut reaction of terror. Anton thumbed his fire selector to full auto and emptied the magazine at the beast. At his six he heard the Warrant Officer do the same.

The bullets did nothing, save for slow the creature's approach and make it look more terrifying.

The *thing* landed beside Anton—just feet away—but he was already diving to create space. A hand with six many-jointed fingers tipped in claws that dripped with black ooze slashed out and tore a graph of lines into the stone. They matched markings on the outside temple wall that Anton thought were decorative carvings. They were signs of struggle. Signs of horror and death. Some of the scratches had looked ancient.

"Changing mags!" the Warrant Officer hollered as Anton got to his feet. Anton was out as well, and he hollered the same just as the winged creature turned its bloody eyes in the direction of the two A-Team officers. It sprang forward, crossing the distance between as easily as Anton might reach for a salt shaker. The Warrant Officer dropped his weapon's bolt home just as the monster punched a hole straight through his midsection, holdings the remnants of his spine in a triumphant claw. The monster-thing screeched in exultation, picking the soldier up with strength that was beyond superhuman. It tossed the man over its shoulder, discarding him onto the skeleton heap as if he were a bale of hay to be fed to the cattle later. Dried bones broke under his weight as he sagged low into the pile. It turned its ire to the still paralyzed Captain that was frozen against the temple's wall.

"Motherfucker over here!" Anton screamed, trying to buy a moment for his Captain to get his shit together. The bat-beast turned to Anton and snarled, spitting out some of the black goo that covered its claws. It sizzled and hissed when the substance hit the stone. "Captain! Get your fucking gun in the fight!"

The Captain's eyes galvanized suddenly, and he lifted his weapon. A moment of error nearly cost them both their lives as the officer squeezed his trigger with the weapon on safe, but a reflexive thumb twitch remedied the issue as the gargoyle lowered its head and charged at Anton. The Captain's weapon barked out a stream of 5.56mm rounds, every third a burning tracer.

This time, the monster felt the sting. Anton's memory was good, some called it great, but sometimes he wished he could forget how easily he could recall the creature ignoring so many of the bullets in that moment. It was in his mind in slow motion from then 'til death, and he hated it. But he loved how those third, white-hot phosphorous tracer rounds bit into the blackened skin and flesh of the thing that had tried to kill him. Bright red blood spilled out of the punctures in its side as it was riddled with the Captain's rounds.

The monster collapsed to the floor at Anton's feet, bleeding a sickly red blood that looked far too thick for any heart to pump. It twitched and squealed a wet noise of death. The smell of it got into Anton's nose as the gunfire died down outside. He fought down a gag.

"Tracers. It couldn't handle the tracers," The Captain said to Anton, now very lucid and back in control.

"No shit. I wish we'd all loaded them up. I think those fuckers led us here Captain. A sacrifice. I think some of those bodies are Australian 1st Commando. I can't tell, but what the fuck?" Anton was angry as he slapped a fresh mag home.

"What the fuck is happening outside?" The Captain replied. He thumbed his helmet microphone and started to hail the other men still outside but stopped when something small and metallic rolled across the floor between the two soldiers. "Frag out!" The officer screamed as he dove flat to the floor, facing the wall. Anton put a stone pillar between the grenade and his body just in time as the explosion happened. His ears rang, his mouth tasted metallic and he was enveloped in a cloud of dirt as well as a mental fog. He watched as three more grenades skittered across the floor like strange little grapefruits, straight over the edge of the first step and down into the pile of bones. Anton dove this time, and narrowly avoided being perforated by the metal and bone shrapnel from the repeated grenade detonations. But he survived. And he was ready as the Indonesians came in to finish what the demon had not.

Three of the eight Asian special operators came in and saw the Captain on the floor, still. They focused on his body a second too long and Anton was able to cut them down with a trio of short bursts from his weapon. The gunfire was deafening in the tiny Candi, as was the smell of demolished bowels, monster gore, and spilled human blood.

Anton got a grenade free and tossed it out the entrance of the temple after pulling the pin. The Captain rolled over and Anton gave him the thumbs up. The grenade boomed outside, loud but considerably quieter to his ears than the four that had gone off in the temple. As soon as the explosion finished, the two Green Berets assaulted out the door, moving as one.

The remaining five Indonesian turncoats were dead in the span of three heartbeats. Two had been flanking the doorway and were caught unaware by the grenade coming out of the temple's entrance. They got bellies full of grenade shards, and the other three traitors had hit the ground to avoid being ripped to shreds. The Captain and Anton were able to put several rounds into their backs before they got to their feet, ending the human treachery. The two surviving operators began to search for their fallen comrades. Perhaps they could be saved.

As they found one dead body after another spirits sagged. The young Michigan soldier could taste his anger, boiling and acidic in his mouth and throat. He wanted more vengeance against the people who'd led his friends to their death. He wanted to kill another monster. After checking another of his friend's throats for a pulse and finding none, Anton called out, "Parker is down Captain."

As he finished announcing the death of another friend, the sound of breaking stone broke the stale, hot afternoon silence. The two men turned from their places on the slope of the depression and looked at the tall structure. It wobbled, faltering slightly, as if the root of the building had been shaken.

Intelligence analysts later came to the conclusion that the ancient structure had been weakened by the claws and spittle of the demon, and the repeated grenade explosions. Anton didn't think that was all correct. It was too scientific. He thought it was the worm.

As fast as the strike of a viper, an enormous mouth blasted up through the dense jungle earth at the base of the temple, swallowing the structure whole and sprouting into the air like a plateau being born. The armor-encrusted worm creature was enormous, gargantuan and alien by any measure, and it was able to writhe straight up into the heights of the trees as the lump of the temple slid down its gullet. The two soldiers ran. There was no fighting a creature that large with the weapons they had. It would need airstrikes, and maybe a priest. Definitely a priest.

The worm swayed its building-thick body back and forth like a swollen tendril of evil, smashing down the trees around the temple, flattening anything that it came into contact with. It wriggled and ruptured the earth, causing destruction on a bomb like scale. Anton had run with all the might his heat depleted body could muster, and he was still almost crushed by falling and flung trees. His Captain narrowly escaped as well, both men cut and punctured by shards of wood. The two men converged hundreds of meters later as the worm retreated down into the gaping hole it had created under the temple. The ground shuddered.

"What the fuck was that?" Anton had asked, hands on knees, bile in his throat.

AT LEAST HE'S NOT ON FIRE

"One of those worm things from the temple carvings. Sweet Jesus. We need to get word to…" The Captain's voice trailed off, and he looked to the hole in the ground. It was easy to see the site of the former temple. The worm had cleared the entire hillside. Anton turned and watched as a black tide of winged monsters vomited forth, streaming into the sky like the a fecal burst of the most evil beast imaginable. Hundreds, then thousands, then more came out. A flowing nightmare spread out into the sky. The men ran again.

It took mere hours for the second hole to open up that day, that time in China. The Chinese weren't prepared, and thousands died by the hour. The third hole appeared in Africa, near the coast in Liberia. The entire nation was wiped off the Earth by sundown, leaving no more than bloody streaks on the ground behind. More holes appeared in South America, then Louisiana and Florida, then Spain and Russia. By week's end there were nearly three dozen of the holes. Hell Holes the media called them. The name stuck.

It took that much time and more for people to realize the greatest weapon against the creatures was fire. That was why the tracer rounds worked so well. White phosphorous burns awfully hot, and works immediately on the winged ones. They were easy, the fliers. They weren't smart, feral and bloodthirsty to a fault, and even though there had been tens of millions of them, they were fragile. Glass cannons. Small arms tracer fire or a flaming arrow proved to be enough to take them down. A few well timed thermite grenades could take out a worm, but you needed to get real close for that to work. Regular bombs were hit or miss literally. Sometimes you could drop napalm on the massive creatures, when they weren't swimming through the cities, toppling buildings from underneath, killing men and women by the thousand. Nowhere was safe.

Against all odds the humans were winning. Surviving. Coming even against the things from below. Some of the holes had been plugged. Nukes dropped down them, and the tops sealed with mountains of blessed concrete. Turns out having a priest nearby wasn't the worst idea. There was some hope returning. Just a little, but it was something.

Anton's Captain was gone. He'd met his end when a flock of the gargoyles attacked their refuge in the outskirts of Brisbane. Through a wall of gunfire in the sky the Captain had been carried up into the clouds and torn in half. His guts had fallen like a knot of bloody string.

Even still, his friends all dead, Anton kept in the fight. He sat in the back of a Blackhawk chopper as it circled a run down neighborhood of Sydney. Beautiful Sydney, ruined by the demons. One of the giant worms was below, a small one by all accounts, only a hundred feet or so long, slithering its massive girth down a neighborhood street, smashing down house after house, trying to find the soft, juicy human morsels inside.

Anton had a team of men with him, and the plan was the same as it always was; to put down near the worm, and kill it before it ran the entire neighborhood into the ground. Some of his men were experienced, with grim faces set to the task they might not return from. Others not as much, their faces shaking, their hands trembling, words of regret held in their mouths behind shut teeth. It didn't matter now. All they needed was the will to fight against the forces of Hell.

And fire. They needed lots and lots of fire.

Tesser: A Dragon Among Us
A Reemergence Novel

Quite the mouthful that title is, eh? But it deserves it, I feel. Tesser was the third major literary undertaking I embarked on. It's a departure from the darkness that's occupied so much of the two projects that predate it, and it is a big step in a new direction for me.

It was a good idea. It IS a good idea.

It was a pleasure to write, and I really feel like it's the best thing I've written. As I write this Tesser is about to be released into the world, so we'll see if this hope turns into sales reality. I'd like to believe it'll catch fire, and sell madly well (or at least as well as AUD does) so I can keep doing this whole 'career as a writer' thing.

But we'll see. Hopefully this taste of his world will entice you to pick up the entire book and discover just what is happening in the world Tesser now calls home.

The book's idea came from my time growing up, similarly to the AUD storyline. One of my besties, Alan MacRaffen, was a fellow dungeon master, and he ran a game for me where I was able to play a dragon that woke up in modern day New York City. We were only able to play a few times, and the campaign was lost to growing up. This book was my opportunity to write the ending to the story he and I started together. Alan if you read this, I hope I did you proud. I know some (read: most) of the details of our campaign have been changed to suit my plan, but I hope you find this story entertaining.

CHRIS PHILBROOK

Tesser is the story of an ancient and benevolent dragon that wakes up deep beneath Boston. He's been asleep for millennia, and has no recollection as to why when he opens his eyes. Very quickly he uses his magic to shift forms to observe on humanity, and what he sees disturbs and angers him. Technology is everywhere, magic is fading faster than the sun at sunset, and perhaps worst of all... he realizes that one of the other dragons is missing.

That wouldn't be that big of a deal, except...

Well, you should just read the story. Here's a taste of the beginning of Tesser: A Dragon Among Us.

Enjoy.

Prologue:
The Dream

I am flying.

I have done this before, many times, and it is joyous.

I feel the gusts buffet my body left and right, up and down. Though the wind is reckless, it isn't violent. I feel the energy of the air lift me higher and higher, through the cool mist of a thick cloud that clings to my face and invigorates me. It is much like the first inhalation of the ocean's air after a long journey to the coast.

Far below me, I see green grass, lush treetops, and grey pebbles poking through the skin of the world. There is a single brown line of disturbed earth winding forward that I know to be a human road. I have flown over it many times before, and I have walked it as well. It is familiar to me, but I cannot quite place where it has come from or where it is leading.

It doesn't matter. I have eyes that see, ears that hear, and a nose that smells. In time, I will discover everything. When I flex my wings and dip below the clouds like a descending sparrow, I can see that miles ahead the road rises on a hillock and ends at a tall wooden gate. Fortified wooden walls spread in both directions. At the center, a majestic castle made of stone and timber sits in stark contrast with the surrounding hovels of mud.

I think it is my castle, but I don't live there. It is mine in the same way that a King owns a dog. Or a Queen owns a King.

My dream is almost over. I feel it like a blue dawn rising on the edge of a long night. It has been a good dream for the most part, though in life, no matter how much the sun shines, storms always appear now and again. It is natural, unstoppable; it is the way of the world. It is the way of my kind.

I sense that I have been dreaming this dream a very long time. More than a night, or a week, or even a year. Centuries have passed, maybe a millennia since I last lay open eyes on the waking world. The castle I am soaring towards in my dream is certainly gone, buried underneath centuries of revolution and crumbled empires.

These thoughts do not cause me alarm. Nor do I fear what the world will be like when I open my eyes soon.

I am beyond mortal fears.

Those that wear two skins are but a nuisance to me.

My skin breaks the teeth of those that drink blood and stalk the night.

Were it not for the teachings and lineage of my kind, the magi would be ordinary, not the wielders of primordial might that they are.

Goblins, monsters, and fae are my kind and they pay me the respect that is my due.

I am the bringer of death from high above.

I am the giver and shaper of life in so many forms.

I am the bringer of light that illuminates all darkness.

I am the stone that cannot be broken and the blade that cannot dull.

I am the legend your grandfathers were told by their grandfathers.

My footsteps shake the ground like the war march of a hundred legions.

My heart beats as the thunder shakes the sky.

If this body does not suit me, I will change it and become whatever will thrive in the soil of the times in which I awake.

I am Tesser, and I am a Dragon.

And as I arc my wings once more to soar above the clouds, my mind elevates me away from my slumber; my fear finally makes itself known. A question, a single nagging lost memory, occurs to me.

Why did I allow myself to be pacified in sleep for so long?
Long slumbers are not my way.
Acquiescing is not my way.
I think I'll find out why I have slept so long now that this dream, this long, long dream, is over. And those that have seen to my sleep had best have had good reason for my time lost.
Because I am Tesser, and I am Dragon.

Chapter One
Abraham "Abe" Fellows

BEEP! BEEP! BEEP!
Is that a car?
BEEP! BEEP! BEEP!
Nah, it sounds too electric.
BEEP! BEEP! BEEP!
God, I hate technology.
BEEP! BEEP! BEEP!
Ha! "God," that's a good one. I don't think Mr. Doyle would approve of me referring to God.
BEEP! BEEP! BEEP!
Why am I sitting in the coffee shop? Where is that infernal beeping coming from? Why does this latte taste like old chewed meat? Or is that a sock I taste?
BEEP! BEEP! BEEP!
Oh Hell, that's my alarm clock. Coffee shop is just a dream. Oh Hell, it's bright out. Damn it, my hand is asleep again. Fingers are number than ever. I'll be fumbling with this shut off button for five minutes now. That Indian asshole in the apartment above me is going to start screaming again.
BEEP! BEEP! BEEP!

I'll cast a spell. I know that cantrip well enough, and my fingers can be as numb as they want.

BEEP! BEEP! BEEP!

Abe sat up on the edge of his worn mattress and addressed the phone sitting on the milk crate he used as a bed stand. The air stirred slightly as the young man gathered his thoughts to cast the spell. There was some magic in the air here in his apartment, his sanctum. On the mantle of the nonfunctional fireplace, he'd organized semi-precious stones that had mystical powers. There was always the scent of incense on the nose. Scents had power.

I'm ready. Abe gestured with his tingly, stiff fingers at the touch screen of his cell phone, still sitting a couple of feet from his hands on the plastic crate. He slid his finger in the air and spoke a word laced with arcane power: "Commoveo."

Abe watched as the image on the phone glitched. The LCD screen didn't feel the touch of his spell in the same way it would've felt a finger made of flesh and blood. He sighed at his newest failed attempt to mix technology and magic. The tingling in his fingers had abated, but he couldn't abandon the spell.

BEEP! BEEP! BEEP!

Fucking thing. "Commoveo," he said again, sliding his fingers through the air, this time with more emphasis and focus. Abe felt a surge of energy come from somewhere and fill his word and fingers with a different tingle altogether.

The red button reacted. Jumped. It slid across the screen smoothly to the other side, silencing the horrid alarm.

BEEP! BE—

"What the hell?" Abe said aloud, running his hand through his thinning black hair. He looked down at his fingers, his palms, turning his hands over several times, trying to find the source of the sudden energy he'd somehow tapped into. He stood on creaky morning legs and looked about his apartment for something new. Perhaps some creature or artifact that Mr. Doyle had perhaps slipped in

AT LEAST HE'S NOT ON FIRE

while he was asleep.

But there was nothing. Just empty pizza boxes, clothes in need of a washer, and Magic the Gathering cards.

His phone elicited another electronic bleat and Abe had a sudden pang of failure. But he was wrong. This was just the ringer. He picked the phone up with living fingers and looked at the caller ID on the screen. It read simply: Mr. Doyle.

Abe thumbed the answer button over and lifted it to his ear. "Mr. Doyle?"

An older British man's voice came back, "Abraham."

"Yes, Mr. Doyle? What can I do for you this morning?" Abe asked quickly. Mr. Doyle didn't like it when he hesitated. Mr. Doyle said men who wanted to learn the art of magic should always act with confidence.

There was a pause on Mr. Doyle's end. *Is he at a loss for words? Has the apocalypse come?*

"Abraham, I think you need to call in sick to work. Someone else will need to tend to your company's accounting today. In fact, you should phone them that you can no longer work for them. Something rather large is afoot in the world and your time needs to be redirected to more appropriate tasks." Doyle sounded somewhere between ecstatic and horrified. Abe had never heard him speak in such a way.

How the hell will I pay rent? "How the hell will I pay rent, Mr. Doyle? I can't afford to quit my job at the firm." Doyle was an accountant at a large law firm. Emotionally, it was a dead end position, but financially it was a homerun, despite the contrary evidence of the décor of his apartment. Abe looked down sadly at the milk crate again.

"Abraham, I can afford for you to be in my employ. Many of my earlier years home in *The* United Kingdom were fiscally bountiful. I shall replace your salary in its entirety. Sack yourself via the telephone and come to my brownstone immediately."

Abe smiled. This was what he had wanted all along. He'd

been an apprentice to the old British mage for nearly two years now, and all he'd learned was three minor spells and how to read ten ancient and long since dead languages. By this point, if the magic thing didn't work out, all he had left was counting beans in a cubicle.

"Abraham, is this arrangement sufficient?"

Shit, I must've gone silent daydreaming again. "Yes, Mr. Doyle. Sorry. Lost in thought. I wanted to tell you I was able to cast a cantrip a few minutes ago. It seemed far more powerful than anything I've ever done before. I think I'm getting the hang of it."

"Dearest Abraham, something else is happening. Something large. Something that will certainly have rippling effects on the whole world, both mundane, and magical. Some of my most precious possessions in my study have begun to... awaken, shall I say. Clocks ticking, candles burning again, things of that nature. All roused by something, or someone."

Abe started to wonder what that meant but caught himself. Daydreaming was unbecoming for someone who wanted to master magic.

"I guess I'll quit and head over then," Abe said softly. *I'll need to go in to get the stuff out of my cube.*

"You guess? I suggest you stop guessing, *Mister* Fellows, and start being confident and assertive. I haven't lived as long as I have to waste my time on someone who guesses at things. Come over when you are ready. And please don't forget to turn your alarm off." Doyle cut the call.

Abe let his hands settle in his lap. He looked around the room, wondering what had happened that made Mr. Doyle ask him to make such a huge change to his life.

BEEP! BEEP! BEEP!

The beeping startled Abe, and he dropped the phone to the hardwood floor of his apartment. He reached down to pick up the smart phone and laughed as he thumbed the snooze button permanently.

"How did he know my alarm wasn't off?"

Chapter Two
Tesser

I am buried in earth.

Tesser's body was immense. From the tip of his nose to the end of his tail, he was nearly one hundred and fifty feet long, fully half the length of a modern football field. Right now he was coiled in tightly, wrapped up to be as small as was physically possible. Tesser had no idea what modern football was though. Not yet at least.

How did I come to be here?

The earth holding Tesser's draconic body still was pressing down with enough force to crush coal into diamonds, but his ancient scaled skin held firm. Dragon flesh would not succumb to something so natural and primal. The mere presence of earth —no matter how crushing it may be- wasn't enough.

I need to reach the surface.

Tesser's eyes were already closed against the dirt and stones, but he furrowed his massive brows tighter and focused his mind. A swirl of sensations cascaded over his awareness as he opened up to all the information the world offered him. One by one each of the scales on his body registered what was against them, and precisely how much pressure existed. His nostrils, still sealed with a flap of scales to keep out the invasive sand, opened a slit and took in the tiniest amount of matter. The scent of organic matter told him his depth. Within seconds Tesser realized which direction was up, and how far he had to burrow to get to the surface.

The muscles that corded the length of Tesser's body were unlike anything science had ever seen. Only the dinosaurs were comparable, but to compare a Tyrannosaurus Rex to Tesser was akin to comparing a garden trowel to a nuclear weapon. Both were capable of moving earth, albeit in a spectacularly different fashion.

Tesser's enormous hand opened, the fingers as large as tree trunks and tipped with curving black scythes of claws. The black tips ripped through the earth smoothly, loosening it in handfuls large enough to fit a small car.

Still too tight.

The immobile body of a dragon might register as stone to a geologist. The bones and muscles are far more dense and supernatural than simple flesh, and when several hundred tons of dragon chooses to move, anything preventing that from happening gives way.

Tesser shrugged. The earth moved. Boston's Back Bay felt it. The media that night reported a "minor tremor," a localized earthquake that reached 2.1 on the Richter scale.

The earth below gave way abruptly. Tesser's massive arms and legs shot out and arrested his short slide. Several yards of stone, some of it shaped in an unnatural way, fell away below him. Tesser immediately opened his nostrils and inhaled for the first time in thousands of years. He was assaulted by foreign smells that caused discomfort. Primarily, he disliked the burning smells, sulfurous and unpleasant, that reminded him of the raw eruptions of volcanoes and the ancient pits of tar that swallowed so many creatures hundreds of thousands of years prior.

Tesser's opened his eyes. Larger by far than many eyes to ever have gazed on the world, these eyes were orbs of gold and slit like a cat's. He could see in any level of darkness, complete blackness if need be. Presently, he looked down through the hole he'd made to the strange passage below. In the oddly lit passage, he could see a uniformly wide channel with three metallic rails running along. One rail hummed with an invisible energy that was oddly reminiscent of magic. Tesser was intrigued. The opening was small, only a third of his length. He would have to shift to a smaller form to fit through.

Tesser was not limited to a single form. The body he found most natural, that of a massive, winged dragon was not his only choice. Tesser could take on the form of any living creature should he wish it and right then he wished to be smaller.

It was a form of magic, though not a spell. More ancient than the clumsy arts the tribal humans were just now grasping. Tesser employed magic the way a bird would fly, or the way a fish swam. It was natural and happened without thought. Tesser shrank down into a form that would fit through the hole below him, starting with his hindquarters first. As his tail and hind legs compacted down, he dug his claws into one side of the space in which he had been dormant, clutching tightly so as not to fall. Once he had reduced to a little less than a third of his original size, Tesser unclenched his still massive claws and descended down until he fell, straddling the channel in the strange stone passage.

The sides of the fairly round tunnel were covered in small, straight shaped white stones that were uniformly smooth. Spaced every so often were images, clearly made by something that could write or draw. It took only a moment for him to realize there were strange images of humans as well.

The images were massive, far larger than the humans he remembered. The largest human he'd ever seen was a savage in a cold village in the far north. He was nearly as tall as Tesser's largest finger and claw. He was a specimen and Tesser was glad to let him live after he threw a spear ignorantly at him. Needless death was not Tesser's way and the man would be good breeding stock to improve the human lineage.

But these humans were a head taller than the warrior had been so long ago. That human came from a village that had only just begun to make markings on hide to remember things. But these images with the large humans...

They have languages. And they are writing now. And some strange magic that allows them to capture perfect images of themselves. I must have slept a very long time indeed.

Tesser heard the small sound of tiny feet moving from the darkness nearby. He'd heard the same sound before, and when he turned, he smiled. One of his favorite of creatures ever had come out to greet him.

A dark-furred rat scurried out, completely unafraid of the massive dragon crouched in the alien tunnel. The rat had come from a hole in the white stoned wall and sniffed emphatically, wriggling its tiny nose and whiskers, taking in the powerful scent of the dragon.

Another sound came from far off down the tunnel, and even though Tesser didn't know what the sound meant, he knew what creature it came from.

A human. I need to observe. I need to see this new world. Unseen.

Tesser shifted forms again.

By the time the MBTA security guard arrived, Tesser had taken the form of a second rat, though his tiny eyes were still golden. He stood fearless, his nose wriggling as emphatically as his new friend's had been a moment before.

The guard reached up to his shoulder and spoke. Tesser didn't understand any of the strange words and thought his manner of dress strange. He wore dark colors, none of which were the skins of an animal like the humans had worn when he was last awake.

"Tunnel collapse, big time. We're gonna need to shut down the Green Line heading west between Copley and Hynes. Holy shit." The T was halted for several hours;

unfortunate morning commuters were forced to find alternative routes.

Tesser cocked his head and realized there was much he had to learn. He had all the time in the world in which to do it. As the other rat darted back into the hole in the wall, he decided to join him. The shrunken dragon would start with the lesson of the rat's tunnels.

Rats always knew how to get around.

Chapter Three
Matilde "Matty" Rindahl

Matty was on the phone.

"Relax, relax, Matty. Your parents love you, and I know you're nervous they're here visiting from Norway, but there's no reason to be all amped up about it," Max said softly from the other side of Boston.

Easy for you to say, Matty thought. "I know, Max, but this is the first time I've actually seen my mom and dad since the miscarriage, and since you and I stopped seeing each other. I guess I'm just freaking out for no reason. Maybe it's that silly little earthquake earlier. Stupid collapsed subway tunnel. Thanks for talking with me."

"It's my pleasure, babe. You know I'll always be your friend," Max said.

His sincerity was sickening. He probably always would be her friend, despite their past year of awkwardness and pain. There had been physical pain as well as emotional pain. Matilde and Max had been engaged to marry, and she pregnant with their baby boy. Money was accumulating in their joint savings account for them to buy a condo in Boston near Boston College where Max was an assistant professor in the psychology department. Matty was a promising grad student with job offers lining up. Matty was a fair-skinned, dark-haired beauty with bright green eyes; Max was tall and lean and handsome. Their lives looked bright and full of inevitable happiness.

The fairy tale unraveled in the morning sun late the summer before when Matty awoke to find a large slick of blood between her legs. Max had rushed her to the hospital, and after the emergency room did everything it could, she was told her baby boy would never draw breath. She had miscarried.

Try as they might, they could not conceive again. A fertility specialist, paid for by Max's family's wealth, told her that she was no longer able to have babies. She was devastated. Max's dream had always been to be a father, and she knew that with her his life would never be complete. There were more than a few tears, but in the end they agreed it was best to go their separate ways, wishing each other love and good luck.

Max returned to work, and soon after, met Amanda, a beautiful grad student not too unlike Matty (though blonde), and they were forming what looked to be a good life. Matty had returned to grad school, this time at Boston University instead of Boston College, and was about to graduate. The reason for her family's visit from Norway was for that graduation.

She realized Max had said something. "What, Max? I'm sorry. I'm all discombobulated right now."

Max laughed, "You should've studied linguistics. You love all those big words. I just said that Amanda and I would try and stop by the graduation tomorrow. I'd like to say hello to your parents if there's time."

Matty winced, "Max, I'm not sure my father is up for that. He's still a bit resentful about the breakup after we lost Aiden." *Aiden. It would've been such a pretty name for a young boy.*

AT LEAST HE'S NOT ON FIRE

"I thought you'd talked to them about it? Explained the whole situation? That it was mutual?" Max sounded genuinely disappointed: more evidence of that sincerity that made her queasy.

"Yes, I did explain everything, Maxwell, but he's my father, and no matter what I say, you'll always be the man that left his daughter after her baby died. If you cured cancer, he'd still never shake your hand again."

Max sighed. "I understand. That's sad. I guess maybe we'll just mail you a congratulations card instead. I'll pick you up a gift certificate to Legal. Can you tell your mother I said hello at least? Does Lindsey hate me too?"

"No, she understands far more than my dad does. I'll pass along your good wishes, Max. I've got to go shortly. I need to drive to Logan to pick them up. Their flight was delayed a little, but I don't want to hit traffic on the way over."

"Yeah, the Storrow will be a bit of a bitch at this hour. Why don't you just take the T over?"

Matty had to swallow a laugh. "My father shouldn't have his slacks dirtied by the seats in Boston's public transportation system. Besides, I want to drive my new car over and show them how well I'm doing. He'll appreciate the new car."

"How is the new job? I was pleased to hear you got the job ahead of getting your master's."

Matty's inner-joy surfaced. "It is outstanding, Max. I love working in the lab, and culturing all the cells, and running all the experiments and trials and all that nerdy stuff. Plus, the money is ludicrous. If I can save like I think I can, then I'll be a very early retiree."

"Take that Italian vacation we talked about. That's terrific, Matty. Well go get your parents. Tell your mother I said hello, and your father too if he doesn't curse me out too much."

"I will, Max, and tell Amanda I said hello," Matty was as sincere as Max. She wanted him to be as happy as he could be, even if that meant it was without her.

"I will. Good luck tomorrow, and toss that cap as high in the air as you can!"

They said their goodbyes and Matty ended the call. The long-legged young woman walked around the island in her new Beacon Hill apartment and spied all the boxes she'd not yet unpacked. Emptying the boxes would be golden busy work for her father. She'd also intentionally left some Ikea furniture unmade; he'd start tackling it all as soon as they walked in the apartment door. That'd give her and her mother time together. She missed her mother fiercely since her and her father had moved to Norway. Her dad had missed his native country fiercely, and her mother was looking for a new experience anyway.

Matty sighed and scooped up her new car keys from the dish on the island. The traffic could be tough with everyone getting out of work, and she didn't want her father to wait any longer than was necessary.

Chapter Four
Tesser

The world was different. Wrong.

When last I wandered the world, the only things that man had made that reached towards the sky were squat towers made of logs and stones errantly piled up, held together by the hopes and dreams of immature minds. These creations, these new structures, are made of stone, glass, and iron and reach nearly to the clouds. They've sprung up like evil weeds, giant and infecting the earth.

These humans remind me more of lice than men.

I'm being bitter. So very bitter. I really do not know what these people have been through since I was sent to slumber.

I've remained in the form of the large rat. It has proven itself indispensable for moving about this settlement. Although, I feel the term settlement is inadequate. I sat in the shadows at high noon in a narrow stone alcove a few days ago and counted over ten thousand unique human faces as they walked by, oblivious. It is quite shocking to me to see all the different skin tones, facial features, and the range of size. When last I dealt with humans they were segregated geographically by design and had multiple distinct lines. Now they are clearly interbred, larger, and obviously smarter. It appears that their natural crossbreeding has been beneficial. This is a good thing.

And the languages! Some letters that are written on signs or on paper look familiar to me, but I've yet to piece anything together. I've learned none of the different spoken dialects, but I believe I've identified five different tongues. I'll learn the most common language soon. I've got a passion for communication.

Tesser's rat body paused in the orange light from the streetlamps high above. Towering buildings, ten, twenty stories tall loomed above like inorganic, steroidal sequoias. Several other rats froze solid as the alpha rat considered the world around him. Inside a nearby building, the bass from a club that had just opened for the night started to rumble. Tesser's rodent head started to bob slowly to the electronic beat.

I must admit, the music they have created is enthralling. All across this settlement I've listened to songs created by stringed instruments, as well as metal horns, and varying other tools to make sound, but this rumbling, thumping, grinding music that comes from this chaotically lit building is my favorite thus far. It has energy. Life.

Tesser resumed his trot down the alley and the other rats unfroze. Even in this relatively alien body, the creatures of the city were blatantly aware that he was in charge. A calico alley cat ten paces away that had been stalking a different, ordinary rat hissed at Tesser as he approached, though it dared not attack. Tesser paid the feline no mind and continued on his way. The fur on the back of the cat's neck stood on its end as Tesser marched past it, unworried. Only when he turned the corner towards a well-lit area of the city did the cat return to its hunt. It understood the food chain.

I must try more of the food. So many culinary delights have been made here. I've eaten out of nearly every refuse container in a wide radius the past two weeks, and no meal twice. Some of it is fetid, and clearly not made of natural ingredients, but some of it is quite delicious. Sometimes, no matter how much of it I've eaten, I'm still hungry.

The thought of the exotic human food made his rat stomach growl eagerly. Tesser did the equivalent of a rat smile. Up ahead, at the end of the long alley that spilled out into the area of Boston known as Chinatown, three people stood talking, their voices rising in volume and anger. A woman had two men surrounding her, one on each side. She was shrinking lower and lower, trying to make herself smaller, trying to escape the building wrath of the men.

I wonder what makes humans angry now?

Tesser picked up the pace. He wanted to be close, to watch, smell, and learn. Examining people in all their heightened emotions was fascinating for him. He couldn't tell what they were saying, but he listened anyway.

The girl spoke, the presence of worry in her voice thick and strong: "Look, guys, I don't really know you all that well. I don't want to go back to your apartment. The night is early. Let's go into Pandemonium, get some drinks, and dance first. See what happens."

She is attractive. Her manner of dress reveals quite a bit of flesh.

"Look," the taller of the two men said. Tesser noted that as he spoke his mouth sounded… loose. Uncoordinated. "We've seen you like, three, four weekends here now, and we've bought you like, ten, twelf drinksh each. We put in our money and our time. Come back to our place, and we'll have some fun there, shugar tits."

She is frowning. Whatever he said did not appeal to her.

The shorter man behind her reached up and put two strong hands on her upper arms. She flinched as his stubby fingers pressed into her flesh. It would leave a mark.

"Look hoe, we're walking," he said brusquely as he moved her deeper into the alley, straight towards his little rat body. Tesser noted that both men had lumps in their clothing where their genitals were. He did not need to speak the language to understand what was going to happen. They were going to rape her.

A complex series of thoughts ran through Tesser's mind as he considered what to do. Almost all sex in the natural world is consensual. Every species that copulates is unconsciously bidden to do so to procreate their line. Saying no is not part of their equation. As Tesser watched the woman's struggle begin, he contemplated the dilemma at hand.

Humans are not the same as other animals. They think, speak, debate, care, and love. For them, with their heavily developed society and ability to use both the ancient magic as well as whatever new magics they have developed to build structures so high, they are set far apart from the rest of the animal kingdom. Yes, there were some animals that raped to intimidate, or to impregnate, but the whole idea of forced copulation for any reason made the dragon's skin itch.

Are this woman's feelings more important than her unconscious need to procreate? Are her emotions on the subject clouding her ability to judge that giving birth is important to further her line?

Tesser's mind raced as the three bodies in front of him moved in slow motion. He watched intently as the woman's face contorted from soft and pleading, to panicked and angry. She fought with all her might against the two men. The young adult males, however, had little panic in their faces. They had lust and anger.

Immediately, Tesser's mind discarded the strange debate as he felt his own emotions flare. This was not about sex. This was about domination. This was about ego. This was not about making a baby, and bringing new, wondrous life into the world. This was about causing pain and evoking a powerfully twisted form of justice. He'd seen it before in many places and he hated it.

And I will not allow it.

Tesser had no designs to shift into his dragon form to stop the rape from happening. His full form would never fit in the alley, and he knew far too little about this world. Revealing his greatest secret now, even for this, would be foolish. He would need to turn into something that would not be out of place.

Tesser became a man.

AT LEAST HE'S NOT ON FIRE

The shift from rat to human was painless, like all other shifts of which Tesser was capable. It took only the thought and desire to become something for him to change into that thing. As a human, Tesser preferred to shift into the same form over and over. It was automatic once he'd become comfortable. Akin to how one might button a familiar pair of jeans in the morning getting dressed, or how it is possible to tie a shoe without thinking about it, or even looking at it. Changing into an unfamiliar body took a few seconds longer as he decided how each and every aspect of his form would appear. What hair? What eyes? How tall?

Tesser's favorite people were the north men. He'd spent centuries amongst them, taking the form of a tall, muscular man. His hair was shorter than was the style then, as he made it now. He copied a hairstyle from a picture he'd seen in a window. His new body was lean and painfully perfect as he took his first steps forward. He was already very close to the men. The odd dark stone felt cool and rough under his bare feet.

The short man with the fat fingers turned and saw Tesser, naked and completely out of place in the alley. He challenged him after a moment of confusion, though Tesser didn't understand his words.

"Fuck off, hobo! Get some fucking clothes!" The man said, passing the frightening woman off to his taller, thinner friend.

Tesser watched as the fat-fingered man curled his hands into fists, preparing for the inevitable altercation to come. Tesser's bright, golden eyes nearly glowed with intensity. The thick person stood his ground, showing more courage than Tesser expected.

"One more step, faggot, and I break your jaw," the fighter said.

Tesser didn't understand him, and even if he had, he wouldn't have stopped. His mind was made. He was a dragon and this was a mere man.

The man angrily stepped into a punch that, had it

connected, would've been powerful. Tesser's draconic brain and reflexes saw it coming long before he even threw it, so when the fist whistled out, Tesser was already stepping to the man's inside with enough time to watch the attempted strike pass by.

The other man and woman watched the entire fight end in the time it took to take a deep breath.

Tesser grabbed the man's right wrist with his left hand and squeezed hard enough to collapse the two bones at the base of the hand. It was the kind of injury that would have resulted in death when Tesser last walked amongst men. Before the man could let loose a scream, Tesser hammered his own fist up and under the man's ribcage, sparing him shattered ribs, but collapsing both his lungs violently. All of the fight had left him and it had only taken a second. Tesser guided the man down to the pavement carefully, though not gently. The man's nose broke against the hard surface they stood on, and he balled up into the fetal position, heaving air back into his empty chest and holding onto his ruined hand as his nose bled out a large pool of red blood. He groaned in pain.

The other man discarded the woman and bolted, abandoning his friend.

Cowardice. I see the humans still can suffer from it.

"Thank you, oh thank you. They were going to rape me," the pretty young woman said, her eyes boiling over with fresh tears of relief. Tesser couldn't understand her, but as she threw her arms around his bare shoulders he knew the essence of what she was conveying. Gratitude. She cried until the man on the ground got his breath back, and started to moan complete words, begging for help.

"Sweet Jesus, please! You fucked my arm up, man! I need help. Call 911! C'mon!" He cried out, rolling around on the ground in agony.

"Go fuck yourself, you North Shore guido! You and your fucking homo friend!" The woman yelled back, clearly out of control. She let go of Tesser and started to rear back a high-heeled shoe to kick the man in the groin.

Tesser again didn't know what she said, but could piece it together. He snatched up her wrists firmly, moving his body between hers and the man he'd just beaten senseless before her kick could reach the hurt man. He made eye contact with her, peering into her blue eyes with his golden orbs.

"Your eyes…" she said softly, entirely forgetting about the man who had planned on attacking her. The gold glittered like its namesake and she was entranced. Her rage melted away.

Tesser knew one word's meaning, and knew already it was nearly universal, and he spoke it softly, "No." He shook his head to match it, indicating that her behavior was too much. She simply nodded, all the will to be cruel gone.

Tesser smiled genuinely, happy that she was safe. He let her wrists go and turned, his long naked body causing the woman to catch her breath. His human form, the same as his rat form, was perfect. Tesser caught the tiniest whiff of her unconscious arousal and smiled. It pleased him enormously.

He crouched low and leaned down to the injured man.

"No, please, man. Take all my money! Take my ring; it's worth three G's! Just don't kill me!" The man scrambled on his back, getting his clothing dirty in the garbage. His shirt was covered in his own blood.

Tesser shook his head in disgust as he stood and walked down the alley, leaving the man and woman behind to sort out their futures. When he could, he stepped behind one of the large metal refuse containers and shifted down into rat form and disappeared. They had seen nothing.

The woman wiped her eyes, smearing her mascara terribly, and reached into her tiny purse for her smart phone.

Chapter Five
Abe Fellows

Mr. Doyle's home was expensive; everything inside it was expensive as well. The Beacon Street brownstone would list on the market for well over five million dollars and that was a fraction of the value of the artifacts that the reclusive sorcerer had stored in it. Where Mr. Doyle had earned the money to own such a home was beyond the young man.

Abe let himself in and walked upstairs. He entered one of the upper floor study rooms and sat at the corner of a long mahogany table. Intricate scrollwork ran along all four edges of the table. Words and runes were delicately carved in a very precise and magically powerful fashion in languages that were spoken no more. The table had been enchanted over a century earlier to be used as a place for experimentation. The spells cast upon it would contain and nullify any accidents, protecting those sitting at the table and the rest of the room. Abe called it "The Error-Proof Table". It alone would fetch half a million dollars at the annual arcane auction in Paris should Mr. Doyle want to sell it.

But the old man would never do that.

His employer sat at the head of the table. The British man had a receding hairline that was quite gray and a round face edged by soft wrinkles. Abe knew that was wrong. The wizard had been slowing the decline of his aging body for some time, and there was no way to tell just how old he was. Mr. Doyle had told tales of experiencing the First World War in person, and that would put his age at no less than a hundred. He didn't look a day older than sixty.

Mr. Doyle sat at the head of the table, leaning over the invisible wall of runes at the table's edge and examining a large pocket watch. The watch was made of gold and, like the table, had its own set of carvings and inset words and runes. Abe watched both the timepiece as well as Mr. Doyle intently, utterly and completely unsure of what was happening. He cleared his throat quietly.

"Shhhh," Mr. Doyle said softly, holding a finger to his lips.

He even shushes in a British accent.

"This watch, this marvel of magical engineering, hasn't worked in nearly ten years, Abraham. Ten years. It has remained in my pocket every day nevertheless. Yesterday, I heard it tick once at precisely noon. If you look at your wristwatch you will notice that we are just a few moments from noon. Your silence will be appreciated, young man."

"Of course. Sorry," Abe replied.

Why do I put up with his attitude? Seriously? I could totally apprentice under a different warlock or sorcerer now. Someone younger, someone with a more modern take on magic. Maybe someone in a west coast coven? Yeah, it might take me a year or two to find someone new, but it might be worth it.

The pocket watch ticked. Abe's eyes had been pointed directly at the second hand, and when it ticked off a single second, there was a brief flare of energy, almost like the watch had vibrated the very reality surrounding it, phasing into and out of our world. Abe felt the hair on the back of his neck stand up.

"Fantastic," Mr. Doyle sat up, pleased like a Cheshire cat. He adjusted his wire-rimmed, circular glasses.

"Does this mean...?" Abe let the question hang in the air. In truth, he had no idea what it meant.

"It means that some of the magic that has faded from this

world is coming back, Abraham. Some of my most trusted associates back in the old world have confirmed that some of the spells and enchanted items that haven't worked in a decade are starting to function again. Powerful magic, Abraham."

Abe looked at the watch, then at his teacher. "What do you think is causing this? Alignments of the stars? A convocation of spellcasters? Some prophecy coming to fruition? Do we have any idea?"

Mr. Doyle sat back in his mahogany chair and wrung his fingers in thought. It was a habit of his. "I cannot say. Most of the prophecies of old are just the ramblings of mad men. Idiots and lunatics that thought they saw the future in tea leaves and the innards of a pig. Whatever has happened, or is happening, is unknown to me as of yet."

"What do we do?" Abe sat back in his own chair and looked through the doorway into a study that was lined wall to wall with ornate glass cases filled with all manner of strange objects. Velvet cases held jeweled rings and bracelets, while hooked mounts displayed swords, daggers, and more than one firearm. That room and all its arcane contents was Mr. Doyle's lifelong passion. All *things* magical were his obsession.

Mr. Doyle sat forward, eagerness in his voice, "We wait, and we watch. Something will happen soon. A sign. A magical portent of the supernatural will arise somewhere, and if we are vigilant, we will see it, and we will move to it and investigate it as the scholars we are, Abraham. I am certain of this. Nothing this powerful happens without leaving a mark, or making itself seen sooner or later."

"Are there divinatory spells we can cast? Can we get out your crystal ball, or fill the scrying pool you've got in the other room?" Abraham's heart jumped. *Oh boy, this will be fun. Real, honest, clairvoyant magic.*

Mr. Doyle shook his head. "I'll see to that, Abraham. That is *my* forte. For now, I need you to do what you do best. I need you to search the internet. YouTube, Twitter, Facebook, and all those other foolish places you frequent so often. Use your modern savvy alongside my magical experience and we will find our clue soon, I suspect."

Are you shitting me? Abe frowned, and spoke before his brain could stop him from doing so, "Are you shitting me?"

Mr. Doyle frowned in a sad fashion. "No, my dear Abraham, I am not 'shitting you.' Swallow your disappointment and get to work, my son. You do your part and I will do mine. Run to the Star Market and fetch yourself one of your energy drinks, and perhaps one of those bags of ranch-flavored corn chips you savor so. Bah. American snacks. We are in for a very long stretch, my apprentice." Mr. Doyle got to his feet with a slight creak to his motion. Abe thought he looked a little older today than yesterday.

"Sorry, Mr. Doyle. I just thought that with all that is happening, I'd play a larger role in the magical side of things. I am apprenticing under you to learn, and this seems like a learning opportunity to me. There isn't much else I can learn about the internet."

Mr. Doyle nodded like a grandfather might and adjusted the waistband on his slate gray slacks. "Abraham, this is a new day, filled with new questions and answers even I can't guess. What I can tell you is that your help with the computer and modern media will be far more effective than you helping me to operate a crystal ball that even at the height of magic and in the hands of an experienced wizard was imprecise at best. You wouldn't want me teaching you how to operate a trebuchet when an assault rifle was available, would you?"

Abe had his own frown now. "No, I guess not."

"Then please go get your snacks and load your assault rifle, young man. We're storming the trenches of knowledge tonight, and hopefully, we'll rout the Krauts soon and find out what has sparked this resurgence in magical activity."

And with that, the old British sorcerer walked away.

"Fuck me," Abe murmured under his breath as he stood up and headed to the stairs.

I'm totally getting a six-pack of Red Bull.

The Vampire of Menlo Park

This one was heart breaking for me. I consider this to be some of my finest short story work, and the anthology I wrote it for was never made. But such is the way when you're a writer. I'm thankful that I was able to have a reason to be inspired to write it though, and that's no small thing.

The Vampire of Menlo Park is a re-imagining of Thomas Edision. If he were a vampire. Certainly would give a powerful motivation to someone to create artificial light now, wouldn't it?

I'd like to do more with this story, or something in the... vein of it, but I don't have a real plan for it at all as of yet. The humor and concept appealed to me, and I feel like it has enough oomph to be more than just this story... somehow. For now, you'll be the first people to read it, and hopefully, you'll see why I thought so highly of it. Make sure you let me know what you thought somehow.

Enjoy.

Thomas Alva Edison 1910: Nature is what we know. We do not know the gods of religions. And nature is not kind, or merciful, or loving. If God made me — the fabled God of the three qualities of which I spoke: mercy, kindness, love — He also made the fish I catch and eat. And where do His mercy, kindness, and love for that fish come in? No; nature made us — nature did it all — not the gods of the religions.

January 10th, 1883
Menlo Park, New Jersey

It was early evening, and a heavy snowfall that deadened the world had just begun outside. A frightfully young intern wearing the best set of clothes his family could afford approached the intricately carved cherry door that marked the entrance to the office of one of the 19th century's greatest minds. His family had sacrificed much for Geoffrey to get this after school job, but in his mind, it was all worth it. The great door was ajar a few inches, and the young man rapped his knuckles hesitantly and adjusted his spectacles before speaking. The door emitted a bit of a creak as he spoke, "Mr. Edison sir?"

The Wizard of Menlo Park was always at work. No matter the hour of the day or night, Thomas Edison was shut into his office, or into one of his basement level laboratories, working on the next scientific achievement that would make the American life better.

"Geoffrey, you may enter," Edison responded.

The pre college intern took a deep breath and pushed the ornate door in, stepping a few feet into the wide and deep office. He stopped ten paces from the massive desk where Edison sat, sipping on a crystal goblet filled with blood red wine. The man was flanked on either side by tall windows that had been shuttered firmly against the light and cold. The room was cool, lit by several of the electric lamps Edison had invented himself, and it reminded Geoffrey of a mausoleum. Edison was only in his mid thirties, with a long, powerful face, bold chin, porcelain skin, and a thick head of dark hair, parted strongly to the left side. Presently he wore a pinstriped vest and a fine cotton blouse, buttoned straight to the neck. He was handsome, and unforgettable. Geoffrey looked in many ways the same as the inventor, though he was sickly. A childhood bout with typhoid fever had stunted his growth, but left his mind untouched. Geoffrey aspired to be a scientist like his idol, Thomas Edison.

"Mr. Edison, sorry to intrude. I came up to tell you that Mr. Bradley asked me to let you know that he's gone home for the night. I've just come from the electric lamp factory. The snow is quite thick." Geoffrey's palms were clammy, and his breath the tiniest bit ragged. Being around Edison made him unreasonably nervous. He looked around to the fine wallpaper and tall bookcases to obscure his thoughts. The office felt cold, but was quite luxurious.

"Very good Geoffrey. Do you have time for me to ask you a few questions young man?" Edison took another small sip from his goblet, leaving a tiny trace of the thick red wine at each corner of his mouth.

"Of- of course Mr. Edison." Geoffrey smoothed out the front of his slacks nervously. It also served to dry the sweat on his palms.

Edison licked the corners of his lips in a strange manner. Geoffrey almost thought it was vaguely sexual. But that couldn't be. "Geoffrey when you stay up late at night, how do your faculties operate? Are you able to function in a scientifically sound manner?"

Geoffrey had to think carefully. He wasn't sure how to answer. "Well sir, I don't typically stay up past nine or ten at night. I've got school early in the morning, and then I come here immediately afterwards. I suppose I would say that if I were to have a task to focus on, I can stay up late and be useful. School studies, for example."

Edison's expression hardened, and he looked boldly at Geoffrey, making a powerful eye contact that Geoffrey couldn't break away from. He felt his heart quicken as Edison's eyes bored into him, evaluating him, rooting him still on the hardwood floor of the office. *The power of the man!*

Edison broke his eyes away after an eternity and lifted the goblet in his large hands once more. Geoffrey noticed for the first time how long and delicate the mastermind's pale white fingers were. Edison swirled the thick wine in the ornate crystal repeatedly. Geoffrey watched as the lush red liquid coated the smooth glass making the shape of a parabola over and over again. Finally Edison put the wine in his mouth and with a single swallow downed the glass's contents.

"I've made arrangements with your parents Geoffrey. Starting next Monday you will be removed from your school, and granted an early diploma. I have need for a late night lab assistant, and if you feel that you can follow my exact instructions, and respect my needs for complete privacy and secrecy, I would like to offer you that position." As Edison finished his statement he leaned forward on the desk, interlacing his long fingers together and resting his powerful chin atop them. His dark eyes—*were they red?*—leveled off at Geoffrey, and suddenly he felt as if he had no choice in the matter.

And he didn't.

"I would be more than delighted sir," Geoffrey said, his voice almost not his own. The young man could swear that Edison was mouthing the very same words along with him.

Edison leaned back in his plush, high backed leather chair and smiled, "Very good Geoffrey. Please take the rest of the week off, and spend some time with your family. Please arrive here at 5pm on Monday. Bring a dinner for yourself. From then on, you will be kept very busy helping me. We have a world to change, after all."

"Thank you Mr. Edison!" Geoffrey said with genuine

glee. "I will do my best to prove my worth to you. I won't disappoint!"

Edison smiled again, "Beware my wrath Geoffrey. Other assistants of mine have later said that I am quite... bloodthirsty. Ravenous, in my needs."

Geoffrey could only manage a series of elated nods. He was beyond ecstatic, and Edison's vaguely sinister tone went entirely over his head.

"Close the door when you leave Geoffrey. Have an enjoyable night, and do be careful in the snow."

"Yes sir, Mr. Edison sir. Thank you again," Geoffrey said as he backed out, pulling the heavy cherry door shut. The sturdy lock caught with a metallic snap and Geoffrey turned around, leaning against the door, grinning ear to ear. He couldn't be happier as he started to walk hurriedly down the hallway to head home. *He was to be Thomas Edison's personal assistant!*

His mind mercifully obliterated the memory of Edison's smile, and the two long fangs that had slipped out through it.

*****

Geoffrey knew that time didn't dilate. It was scientifically impossible for a minute to take longer than sixty seconds, and the same theorem held true for the length of a weekend. However, the remainder of the week that Thomas Edison offered him the job as lab assistant, and the weekend he spent with his family felt like the longest stretch of days that had ever passed on this blue and green Earth.

When Geoffrey entered the building everyone else was leaving for the night. Only the managers and senior staff remained, and they were bundling up against the cold as Geoffrey stripped off his layers. Mr. Bradley, the hawkish, bearded man who worked as one of Edison's manufacturing managers was tightening a scarf around his neck as Geoffrey unbuttoned his sweater.

"You're going to want to leave that on," Bradley said gruffly, fishing around in a tall, pressed copper bin for his walking cane.

"What sir?" Geoffrey asked, his fingers hovering over a brown button.

"Your sweater. Mr. Edison keeps the basement laboratory quite chilly. The colder temperatures serve the experiments he performs down there," Mr. Bradley responded. He pulled an ornate cane from the bin, topped with a carved brass head of a bird of prey. It was beautiful, but had a darkness to it that Geoffrey couldn't quite place.

"What research does Mr. Edison do down there, if you don't mind my asking?"

Mr. Bradley put the tip of the cane to the floor and leaned hard on the brass bird. He searched for an answer for some time, long enough for Geoffrey to button his sweater all the way back up.

"I don't know Geoff. No one really knows. He only brings down a single assistant at a time, and when they are let go, they are sent away to boarding schools, or universities far abroad. Their secrecy is bought with an education, or a bribe. In fact, I've never seen or heard from any of his assistants once they've left his employ in that basement."

Geoffrey swallowed with a very dry mouth. He felt silly for being scared.

"I will say this Geoff, I will not work with Mr. Edison at night. Not since he took ill a few years ago. He's changed. Harsher, colder. Obsessed with lighting the night, fearful of candles in an irrational way. Fire in any form, truthfully. Where are the stoves on this side of the building I ask you? And I couldn't tell you when he last took a meal. He's quite strange now. Be wary boy. Very wary."

"Wary of what? Do you think he's gone mad? Thomas Edison, genius of our age, mad?" Geoffrey was half frightened, and half shocked.

Mr. Bradley leaned in close to Geoffrey. The teenager could smell the coffee on the businessman's breath as he

AT LEAST HE'S NOT ON FIRE

spoke, "I won't be with him at night, and I had this made. Just in case." Mr. Bradley lifted his cane and gave the brass head a twist. The top of the cane came free, and he lifted it, revealing a slender, foot long wooden spike. The tip was as sharp as a pencil's.

"Mr. Bradley that's quite strange."

The older businessman shrugged, and examined his odd tool, "It's made of ash. Ash is a good wood Geoffrey. There's a power in it. Science hasn't shown us why, but many cultures have recognized that. Call me superstitious, but I feel better knowing I have this. Be careful Geoff. You've a bright future ahead of you. I would hate to see it lost. Good evening."

And with that, Mr. Bradley left the warm confines of the building, trudging out in the packed New Jersey snow.

Geoffrey didn't feel much warmer after the door swung shut. A chill had set into his bones that would take a good long time to fade away. He picked up the small black lunch tin his mother had filled for him, and he set off down the hallway to Mr. Edison's office.

*****

The time with Mr. Edison passed quickly. The vast majority of it was mundane when compared to Mr. Bradley's odd paranoia, and soaked through and through with the science that Geoffrey wanted so badly to learn. One sunless night turned over to the next, and one week into another, and before he knew it, the New Jersey winter had given way for the burgeoning warmth of spring.

Geoffrey thought it odd when Mr. Edison asked him to come in later and later as time progressed. First it was half past five for a week, then six, then half past six. It wasn't until Geoffrey realized that his arrival times to the basement lab were only scant minutes after the sunset each day that he felt something was amiss. It couldn't be a coincidence.

It didn't help that in three months of working with Mr.

Edison, nine or more hours at a stretch, all he consumed was glass after glass of thick red wine, all from the same locked cabinet. Not one meal, nor bite of food.

His curiosity could take no more.

"Mr. Edison?" Geoffrey asked in a moment of solitude. The two men had just completed a round of esoteric experiments on filament composition. Thomas was trying to find a bulb filament that would illuminate longer. The search had consumed them of late.

"Yes Geoffrey?" Edison said dismissively as he penned immaculate notes into a leather bound journal.

Geoff sat his own notebook down on the lab counter and took a deep breath before continuing, "I've been your assistant here for several months now. I want you to know I'm thankful, but I have some questions. Personal questions I'd like to put forth, if you don't mind." Geoffrey adjusted his spectacles on the bridge of his nose.

Edison lowered his quill—he favored using an inkwell and quill late at night—and picked up his ever present goblet of red wine. "Previous assistants have asked personal questions Geoffrey. Many of them did not like the answers they received, leading to their resignation, or termination. Ask what you will, but be mindful that the answers you seek might only muddle your feelings." The genius sipped at his wine, and inclined his head, indicating for Geoffrey to speak.

Geoffrey swallowed down yet another dry mouth as his heartbeat thumped loudly in his ears. He steeled himself, and asked his first question, "Why do we only work at night?"

Edison was quick to answer, "I dislike the sun. Also, it amuses me that the research we do to eliminate the darkness of night is done at night. I find it fitting. Poetic."

Geoffrey nodded apprehensively. He didn't quite like that answer, but was scared to press the issue. "I also wondered about your diet sir. We've spent so long together these past few months, and I've never seen you eat so much as a single bite of food. All I've ever observed you eat or drink is that wine sir, and that worries me. How you stay well is mystifying."

Edison cracked another wry grin, revealing teeth stained pink from the wine, "I've found that my stomach has a gentle constitution since I took ill several years ago. I eat very little now, and my wine soothes my humors." He lifted the glass chalice and took another sip to emphasize the point.

"I see. I guess I just- well, I find it odd that we aren't using the larger laboratory upstairs, where the others work, and you avoid sunlight entirely, and you never eat. It's very odd, and I worry."

"Don't fret Geoffrey. I am as healthy as an ox, and I plan on being around forever. If you play your cards right my son, I might just keep you around here for a good long time as well, and you will learn more science than you can imagine. We will change the world! Now, fetch me another bottle of the red please. I seem to have run out." Edison downed the remainder of his glass and motioned for the sturdy wine cabinet in the corner of the low ceilinged room. Bolstered by the distraction of the small task, Geoffrey hopped up and retrieved the last heavy red bottle. He shut the stained glass door to the now empty cabinet, and started walking back to Edison.

"This is the last bottle sir," he said as he walked around one of the larger lab counters.

"Oh dear. I'll need to send for more tomorrow. This bottle should get me through tonight though. Do bring it here. Be careful," Edison snapped his fingers impatiently. Geoffrey thought it looked almost nervous, almost frantic.

Disaster struck. Geoffrey, lost in thought about Edison's near manic moment, cut the final corner near the lab counter too short, clipping the bottom of the bottle on the hard soapstone surface, shattering it. The red wine issued out the broken bottom in a flood, covering his best slacks and creating a substantial spill on the smooth tile floor. The cleanup would set them back the rest of the night.

"Oh no Mr. Edison! I'm so sorry!" Geoffrey said, looking

down at the floor and the red spill. His foot was in the center of the mess, and he turned slightly, causing the foot to skid and slide on the wine. The consistency of it struck him as odd, and he knelt quickly, putting a knee and a finger in the dark red pool. He lifted the red fingertip to his nose, but before he even smelled the coppery, iron filled blood, he knew what it was. He stood, and saw a look that was beyond rage, and something entirely inhuman on the face of his mentor.

"Mr. Edison-" Geoffrey said, suddenly very frightened for his life.

Edison moved—no, Edison *launched* over the lab counter like an enormous predator cat. Geoffrey didn't have the time or sufficient reflexes to move, and literally before he knew it, his head was bouncing off the tile floor, and he was blacked out. When he came back to consciousness, Edison was crouched over his chest with one hand holding his neck against the floor in a grip that was vice-like. Edison looked positively feral, and radiant with rage. Long yellow-white fangs came down where the canines should have been in his mouth, and now for certain, Geoffrey knew Edison's eyes were red. They glowed not unlike the red embers from Edison's light bulbs.

Geoffrey was taken aback by how *cold* he felt against him.

"I SAID BE CAREFUL!" Edison snarled in Geoffrey's face, his mouth stinking of rotten blood. "Now I'll need to feed Geoffrey! And you are the only meal here tonight! What will I tell your parents when you're a husk in a closed casket? Moron!"

Geoff couldn't breathe. Edison's claws were shutting his windpipe, and he gasped and sputtered, trying to say something, say anything that might buy him his life. Finally, as he was about to succumb to the blackness once more, Edison let up the tiniest bit, and the closing circle of death retreated.

Geoffrey coughed, "Mr. Edison, what are you? You're

cold, you've been drinking blood? You- you're a beast!"

The fingers tightened again, "Do not presume to tell me what I am boy. I am primordial! I am advancement beyond humankind, beyond the brittle flesh of the living! I am the first of an old kind to take back the blackness of night. I am a vampire!" Edison snarled, baring the fangs once more.

What was a Vampire? Geoffrey choked out a broken series of words, "What? How?"

Edison looked down to the pool of blood and ran his hand through the spill. Blood red fingers disappeared into his mouth one by one, and he suckled on them like a babe at a teat. The tiniest amount of the vitae seemed to stabilize the monster that had erupted.

"I was approached by a wealthy businessman while on holiday in Europe. He gave me an offer I could not refuse. Eternity to research my obsessions. All I need sacrifice was my life, and the sun. But you see, that is not a loss at all my boy, for I have created *electric light*."

Geoffrey nodded slightly. Edison's hand had loosened more. It seemed like the blood had calmed him. "But you also need to drink blood? Do you kill?"

"Vampires are ageless creatures from beyond the curtain of death young boy. Not human, not alive, but more. Yes, I need to drink blood to maintain my existence. Yes the sun is my bane. Yes I must kill now and again but sacrifices must be made Geoffrey. To advance science you must question everything, even morality, even God. Every soul that meets their end in my red wine glass furthers mankind as a whole. It is a small price to pay, murder."

Geoffrey was nearly speechless. Nearly. "Who dies?" he asked.

Edison was now sitting on his haunches, gargoyle-like, "Anyone at first, when the thirst is strongest. But now, just immigrants. I have several men who offer jobs to immigrants getting off of boats in New York City. A few every week is more than enough. In fact, I'm contributing rather substantial funds anonymously to the creation of a new immigration center. It is to be called Ellis Island. But no one will know I have anything to do with it, right Geoffrey?" Edison's glowing red eyes flared as he looked back down at the young man below him.

Geoffrey shook his head, his eyes fixated on Edison's long fangs, "Of course sir. Nothing you say shall ever pass from my lips. I understand completely."

Edison continued. He was fervent, zealous, "Your predecessors Geoffrey, some were just incompetent, and they saved the lives of immigrants, feeding me instead of the foreigners. But some, like you, asked the questions. You are the smart ones Geoffrey, the inquisitive minds. But are you different from the others? Can you handle the truth of who and what I am and persevere in the face of that reality? For the good of science? For the good of mankind?" Edison looked away, then back again, but with a different kind of smile entirely, "Or will you become just another cabinet of red wine for me?"

Geoffrey nodded emphatically, "Sir I understand. You've given everything to be one of the world's most prolific minds, and I'd do the same. No one can understand what it means to truly seek knowledge in the way you have, and the way I wish to. I would do anything for the world, for science."

Edison's eyes lost their raw flare and faded back to a normal color as he regarded the boy on the floor below him. Geoffrey watched as his eyes drifted down to the throbbing artery in his neck, then back up to his eyes. Edison's fangs slowly retracted back into his gums, much like a cat's claws.

"You seek eternal life?" He asked softly.

"I don't seek eternal life Mr. Edison. I wish to seek. To learn, to study, and to know. If that means I must be as you, I accept that sacrifice."

"You cannot know what you say, you are far too young, too naïve. You have not yet proven yourself loyal enough to receive that gift. You've sacrificed so little. But I shall spare your life for this night. I have a strange faith in you that I

AT LEAST HE'S NOT ON FIRE

have never possessed over my previous aides."

Geoffrey was ecstatic, "Thank you good sir. I shall prove my worth, as I said. I know I will."

Edison stood, the knees of his pants, and his face covered in blood. "I suggest you never drop another bottle of my wine if you wish to live Geoffrey. Quite literally it is the *one thing* that is keeping my teeth from your throat every night."

*****

It took Geoffrey two full weeks of sleepless days to build up the courage to approach Mr. Bradley. He knew it had to be done, and the only man who Geoffrey thought knew enough about Edison's... condition, to be of any assistance.

Geoffrey couldn't fail in this, or Edison would kill him. And drink him.

Mr. Bradley sat in his office, his hat resting on the top of the spike filled cane in the corner. Mr. Bradley wore only his vest, and he was sweating profusely. The early summer heat had risen dramatically, and the assembly line was even hotter. Several of the immigrant workers—those Mr. Edison hadn't drained of blood—called the sweat den the devil's den. Mr. Bradley wiped his brow with a white handkerchief and shuffled some forms on his desk, looking for something in the numbers and words.

"Mr.-, Mr. Bradley?" Geoffrey asked from the doorway. Geoff had come into work far earlier than usual, specifically to meet with the man about Mr. Edison, and his... needs.

Bradley looked up from his sweat stained

paperwork and assessed Geoff. "You've gotten a bit pale Geoffrey. All these late nights with Mr. Edison have taken a toll on your complexion."

Geoffrey laughed nervously, "They've certainly taken a toll sir. Speaking of which, I was wondering if I could steal a few minutes of your time? Regarding Mr. Edison and the... condition you spoke of?"

Bradley sat the paperwork down and stared at Geoffrey. There was an uncomfortable stretch of silence, and Geoff thought Mr. Bradley might've forgotten what he was referring to, or wanted nothing to do with the conversation. Finally he motioned for Geoff to take a seat in the hard wooden chair near his desk.

"What is it you need to talk about?" The plant manager asked, pulling the bottom desk drawer out and producing two tumblers and a bottle of scotch.

Geoff watched him slowly pour a finger in each tumbler, mesmerized by the brown, oaky liquor splashing up the sides of the glass. Finally he spoke as Bradley pushed the drink across the desk to him.

"Mr. Edison has changed sir. Before I started to work with him, something dire happened. Something I think you've suspected all along."

Bradley downed the finger of scotch and immediately poured twice as much into the glass. He swirled it around and licked his lips, "What can you tell me young man? Make no statements that aren't fact. In this manner I suspect there's precious little we can afford to guess on."

"I believe Mr. Edison is a vampire, Geoff said quietly, looking over his shoulder at the open office door. He felt a bead of salty sweat trickle down his cheek. He couldn't tell if it was from the sweltering humidity, or from nerves.

"Where did you learn that word?" Mr. Bradley asked, sipping at the scotch.

"I read it in a book. Mr. Edison also said it a few times. It caught my curiosity so I did a bit of research," Geoffrey replied, sipping at the harsh liquor. It burned his throat as it slid down, and he wondered why anyone would drink it.

"I think you're right Geoffrey. I've wondered for a good long time since Mr. Edison took ill, and since he stopped eating and going out at day. I've also thought it strange how he talks poorly of religion now, saying it's all bunk. I've Romanian blood in me, and my mother and father told me of the blood drinkers. Have you seen him drink his wine? It's blood, isn't it?"

Geoffrey sipped the liquor, and slowly nodded.

"I knew it. I've known all along. He is one of God's forsaken."

"I don't know what to do Mr. Bradley. I accidentally dropped a bottle of his… wine the other day, and he nearly killed me. Teeth as long as a wolf's, and eyes that glowed like coals. He had such strength sir. He held me down like a bear might hold a river salmon. I was able to talk him out of killing me, and since I've been able to stay in his good graces."

"He's a murderer."

Geoffrey nodded, "I think he's been killing people every week since he took ill, as you said he did. What do we do?"

Bradley's hand shook as he tipped the tumbler once more this time draining it. He started nodding, building in rapidity to the point where Geoffrey thought the man might be having a small seizure. Finally he stopped, setting the glass down on the wide oak desk with a clink.

"What do we do sir?" Geoff asked again.

"We kill him, like my ancestors did in Romania, the same way they have for centuries. I will drive my ash stake into his cold dead heart. And to be sure, we shall strike his head from his shoulders, and bury one far from the other. Are you with me Geoffrey? Do you have the courage to do this with me?"

Geoffrey reached across the desk and picked up the bottle of scotch. With shaky hands he poured an inch of the liquor, and downed it immediately, wincing from the scorched throat it gave him. He nodded, almost of a different mind, "Yes Mr. Bradley. I don't see as if I have a different choice in the matter."

The factory manager got up and walked around the desk, closing the office door gingerly. He sat back down, and produced a clean sheet of letterhead paper from a stack. He picked up a pencil, and started to jot notes.

"What are you doing?" Geoff asked.

Bradley looked up and scratched his beard with dirty fingers. Geoff thought there were a few new gray hairs. Quite a few.

"First, we plan."

*****

"He sleeps in a dormitory in the basement," Geoffrey told Mr. Bradley two weeks later. It was then deep into the core of the humid New Jersey summer, and the heat was crushing in the mid afternoon. The sun bored through the slats in the window shade like daggers made of flame. Glasses of iced tea one after another did their best to fight against the dehydration, but it was a lost cause until the sun went down.

Bradley looked over the notes Geoff had written earlier and nodded. They had their plan.

The manager spoke, "My mother once told me that the vampires are weaker during the day as they sleep."

Geoffrey didn't know how to respond, so he nodded. He felt his heartbeat quicken.

"We go now. We do this and end it all. Today, Thomas Edison meets his end Geoffrey, and we will either be hailed as heroes, or criminals should we do this wrong."

"I don't know if I-"

"You've no choice. Take the cane, I'll get the torches. Today, we use only the light that fire provides us. Edison's electric light will not shed justice in this, the good Lord's matter," Bradley stood, and for the first time, the manager looked confident. Righteous. Just.

Geoffrey grabbed the brass headed cane and followed the man out into the hallway towards the stairs that would take them down to where Edison's cold, dark lair was.

*****

Edison's body was in a container that looked exactly like a seven foot long water chest. A large padlock hung from it, but Geoffrey knew it to be false. Like the chest it hung from, it was all only for the sake of appearance. A single ornament designed to dissuade the viewer from the real purpose of the chest.

In his left hand Bradley held the lit torch they had made from a scrap of wood, a handkerchief, and some of the vodka the Russian immigrants from the factory drank so freely. It burned bright and clean, casting orange light and black shadows across the finely appointed apartment. In his right hand Bradley held a large cross. He made the sign of the holy trinity and motioned for Geoffrey to approach the chest with him.

The young man held his breath, his heart hammering away. Adrenaline coursed through him, electrifying his every nerve and muscle, much like Edison's loved energy might. He had never felt so alive, or so close to death. It was a queer exhilaration.

"Open it," Bradley said quietly.

Geoffrey walked around the newly minted vampire slayer and took the torch from him. He handed off the hawk headed cane and with a nod, lifted the padlock, raising the lid of the water chest as well. Bradley had already unscrewed the spike from the cane, and had it at the ready.

"Good afternoon Mr. Bradley," said Edison from the corner of the room, several feet from the chest. His voice was low, and full of malice.

Bradley spun, producing the holy cross at the area of the bedroom Edison had spoken from. Geoffrey lifted the torch to try and shed more light on the vampire, his hand shaking like a leaf blowing in a pre-storm wind. The shadows, impossibly black and thick, peeled away from the corner of the room like a cloak unfurling. The darkness was unnatural, and the torch's flame did little to pierce it. Edison took a step forward into the room, his fangs bared casually. He looked omnipotent.

"In the name of God I command you to hold still unholy beast, creature of the night, Satan's spawn!" Bradley shouted, his voice booming with a religious might Geoffrey was astounded by.

Edison's eyes flared like the torch's flame, and he rooted his feet to the floor. He was held firm.

"I have come to you as an agent of our holy God to end your murderous ways! I shall drive this stake made of ash into your dead, evil heart, and I shall stop this blasphemy of the living order!" Bradley raised the head of the cane high, showing it to Edison as he might show a shard of the holy cross itself. Edison's eyes showed something Geoffrey had never seen, and never expected them to; fear.

"Be gone, foul demon of Satan!" Bradley yelled, and he brought the stake down into Edison's chest.

The wooden stake busted apart against the white shirt Edison wore as if it were made of tissue paper. Tiny shards of wood fell impotently to the floor as Mr. Bradley' hand thumped into Edison's flesh. All that remained in it was the brass hawk's head. The factory manager, full of the fury of his holy God, had done no more than wrinkle the vampire's shirt.

Edison smiled, and wordlessly backhanded the man hard enough to twist his head completely around. Geoffrey stood, open mouthed, watching Mr. Bradley's face contort and twitch, turned entirely around to the wrong direction. Beyond that, he watched as Edison caught the body from falling, and sank his teeth into the limp neck of the dying man. There was a wet, sucking sound as all of the man's vitae was drained from him. It took less time to turn Mr. Bradley into a dried husk than Geoffrey imagined it would've.

Edison dropped the carcass on the floor as he might've discarded a spent cigarette. He looked up at Geoffrey and smiled once more. Geoffrey lowered the torch, and stood his ground, frightened of what would happen next. Edison walked slowly over towards him, stopping when he was mere inches away.

"The cane?" Edison asked.

Geoffrey swallowed. His whole life hung in the balance, and his next words would tip it one way, or the other, "Balsa wood. I switched it earlier today when Mr. Bradley was at lunch."

Edison smiled, "Very clever. I always knew he disliked me. Even before I was turned into a vampire. He was so poor at hiding his faces. A good poker opponent though."

Geoffrey smiled, and beamed.

"Well done my young boy."

"Anything for science Mr. Edison. Anything."

"Make your arrangements for travel. Your parents think you're going to Germany to school. You won't be seeing them again, ever."

"Very good sir."

"It will be nice to have reliable help here in the laboratory Geoffrey. Now all that's left is a body double to pretend to be me. Someone to grow old, and marry, and be seen during the day when I cannot be out and about. We'll start that search immediately after you've become as I am."

"Very good sir."

Edison put his arm lovingly around the young man and the two gazed at Mr. Bradley's desiccated body. "The sacrifices we make for science."

THE WRATH OF THE ORPHANS
- Book One of The Kinless Trilogy -

Many moons ago I was involved in the gaming industry as a playtester, rules designer, and developer. I loved it, but the money was meh, and when the company I was working primarily for was bought out, I was told I could relocate to the west coast for a meager wage, or I could be let go.

It wasn't worth moving, so I set myself free like the proverbial butterfly on the wind, and moved on to the existential crisis brought on by the layoff, the death of my father, and other things that conspire against us each and every day of our lives.

Looking at the bright side of that, while I was in development I had side projects. If you haven't figured out by now that I love role playing games, I do. Pen and paper, video game, you name it, I'll give it a whirl. I own hundreds if not thousands of RPG books, and I've always wanted to design my own. Isn't that every gamer nerd's dream? To create a game for others to enjoy?

Enter the world of Elmoryn. I created the entire world, and hundreds of years of its history for a game that has yet to be made. In fact, sitting on the hard drive of my laptop right now is nearly three hundred thousand words of game rules and glorious content that are more or less ready to go. Someday, I'll get it assembled, and perhaps something will come of it. I'm also happy that I get to create this world with my friend Alan MacRaffen. He does all the maps, editing, and also helps ensure that the world makes sense, and works on levels that my brain can't comprehend properly.

On the heels of AUD's explosion I decided to write novels set in the world I'd grown to love. The Wrath of the Orphans follows the twins Malwynn and Umaryn as they experience the horror of having everything they've known and loved taken from them at the start of a war that they can't seem to escape. Chaos reigns over them, and they are lost to it.

And if you can't escape that chaos, BECOME IT.

Wrath is a dark fantasy. I mean dark. Think Tarantino meets Tolkien. The twins twist, change, and in their pursuit of vengeance they leave no stone unturned, no bone unbroken, and reduce themselves to the very thing they claim to hate so much. Wrath is their journey from top to bottom, and how they claw their way out of the terrible prison of vengeance they've buried and locked themselves under.

As I write this, book one is released, and book two, The Motive for Massacre is about to be released. I'm incredibly proud of this world, the magic of it, and the future it could have if more people gave it a try. As with all fantasy settings, the first few chapters are tough, because they're slower, with lots of world building and required exposition. Once you get past the somewhat drier stuff, the book really takes off.

Enjoy.

- Chapter One -
A Wretched Affair

"We're almost out of time. We need to move faster!" The young man said, panic ripe in his voice. He carried a small woman in his thin arms. Her head hung limp, and the arm not pinned against the man's chest swung to and fro lifelessly. She was dead.

Ahead of him ran his younger sister. They'd just entered the fringe of the small village their farm was on the outside of. New Picknell. Quiet and safe New Picknell. As the son carried the dead body of his mother at a jog, the smaller sister searched out for the single home that would contain their salvation. The home of New Picknell's lone Apostle resident.

"Catherine!" The daughter yelled, her voice cracking from the emotion she'd been expending since her mother's death. "Catherine we need you!" They would have to cross the entire town to get to the small farm Catherine's family lived in. Theirs was a good sized home still inside the town's edge, still protected from solitude and the wilds of Elmoryn.

A woman stood up from her seat at a washboard, letting the wet laundry slide down into the metal basin. She saw the siblings running as fast as they could manage, and her face went pale. She reached down beside the washbasin and produced a mallet. Her lungs inflated to holler a warning, "Dead body in the city! Dead body in the city!" After screaming her warning she clutched the mallet to her chest. Her anxiety decreasing, she retreated to the safety of her home, where she shut the door, and barred it.

As the frightened pair ran through the small village the doors of homes either slammed shut, or swung open with an adult standing in the frame. Everyone was armed, and stared at the body in the boy's arms. They feared it. They feared what it could become. They feared what it would become if their journey took too long.

"Catherine! Catherine!" The daughter screamed again, losing what was left of her already bruised voice. Other voices joined her, sharing the tremendous urgency. The screams of "Catherine!" were nearly deafening by the time they reached the dirt street that ended at the wooden fence that marked the edge of the family farm they had been seeking.

"Catherine please, come quick!" The son yelled, his arms failing. He had been carrying his dead mother for almost an hour at nearly a sprint, and his young body was well past its limit.

His voice pierced the home and a black haired woman opened the door. Her face was calm, reserved, and full of a timeless poise that instantly spread relief to all those in a panic outside her home's fence. As she stepped outside her door and walked down the finely laid stone path to the sturdy gate she moved with purpose, and confidence. Her trip ended just as the daughter and son reached the gate. The Apostle flipped the latch on the gate and pulled it open, motioning for the son to bring the dead body to a stone bench that was curiously placed just off the stone walkway. Its purpose was not for sitting.

"How long has she been gone Nickolas?" Catherine asked calmly, gathering the fabric of her long cream colored dress to her hip. The garment flowed in the warm, late summer breeze. The stink of the dead body hadn't yet come, and inside the yard the only scent was that of freshly cut grass.

The young man, Nickolas, panted as he put his mother's body down on the polished granite slab. She looked very small and almost stately as he arranged her arms at her side. "I don't know. She was hit by a rotting timber in our barn. It fell on her from the hayloft and struck her dead. We found her and came running as fast as we could. The trip here alone was an hour. She could've been dead for a few hours more."

"Where is your father?" Catherine asked in a slow and steady cadence, inspecting the dead body with tender care. She had done this many times, and this was her way.

This time, the daughter replied, her voice almost entirely gone now, "He left early yesterday to bring a small harvest to the rails. He won't be back until tomorrow at the earliest." She coughed a dry cough and shed a thick tear down her cheek.

Catherine winced, "That's a shame. He will be heartbroken, as I'm sure you both are." She put a reassuring hand on the shoulders of the siblings. From the other side of the fence the town's residents that were brave enough to watch had formed a line against the thick wood separating Catherine's property from the town proper. Pitchforks, shovels, hammers, and even a few swords and axes were in their hands. They stared intently at the body on the granite surface just a few feet away.

From the front door of her home a brother and sister duo not unlike the ones that had just delivered their dead mother's body walked out into the yard. The twins were tall, thin, and had hair black like their mother. They both shared clear eyes of a striking blue. They looked on from the step of the home with calm concern.

Catherine reached out and took the hands of the siblings that were now half orphaned. "Everyone gathered here please give the spirit of the recently departed Julianne a few moments of silence while I free her soul from the bonds of flesh that bind her."

Everyone went silent, and Catherine began the service, her hands still clutching to the brother and sister.

Head lowered, her silken voice reached out beyond the veil of death, "All life is fragile. Today we learn that lesson yet again. The life of Julianne has reached its end, and despite the injustice of her being taken away from the world of the living, her legacy does not end today."

Catherine looked up at the body, ensuring it was still on

the slab before continuing, "Julianne's immortal spirit is still within her, and in this moment we shall set her soul free from the body she had in life. She will roam these plains, and these hills forever, lending support to her friends and families and their descendents for all time. She shall hear the praise and adoration of the living as if she were still here. She shall lend Apostles a bit of her very essence, allowing us to perform The Way, and give mystical boons to those we can. In life she gave love and security, but in death she gives so much more, and she will do this forever."

Catherine let go of the sibling's hands as they slowly wept. They'd seen the Blessing of Soul's rest done before, and to complete the ritual, Catherine needed both of her hands. The mother of three reached into a small pocket on the front of her dress and produced a handmade cloth bag. She retrieved a tiny vial of scented oil, and sprinkled a minute amount of herbs down the length of Julianne's dead body. The herbs and the oil were essential components to the blessing Catherine was performing. They physically and tangibly bound her will to the act, and enabled her to use the Apostle's version of The Way, or Elmoryn's magic. Catherine's magic was fueled by her latent talent to access the hundreds of thousands of ancestor spirits roaming the land. In a few moments, Julianne would join them.

When the proper number of oil drops had been applied, and the right amount of herbs placed on the right points of the body, Catherine placed her hands on Julianne's body. The intimate connection of Apostle and body signaled the final moments of the blessing. Catherine reached out of her own body and soul, and into the body of the deceased woman. It was not unlike opening a metaphysical cage, and setting free a bird kept within. Her hands never moved, but behind her closed eyes she felt Julianne's body shudder briefly as her spirit was set free. Her soul would not rot and fester in her body. She would not become the undead everyone gathered feared.

She took her warm fingers from the now cooling body

and reached her full height. The young girl still wept, but when Catherine embraced her, she calmed quickly, feeling the relief the blessing had given them. The crowd gathered gave a quiet round of clapping as the tension faded from the afternoon. They filtered out quickly, letting the family grieve in privacy.

"Thank you," Nickolas said.

Catherine smiled warmly, "You are very welcome. We can store the body until your father arrives, give you time to gather wood for her pyre." Cremated bodies couldn't be animated by rogue Necromancers, no matter how unlikely the chance of that happening was. Tradition was tradition after all, and since The Great Plague almost eradicated all human life from the face of Elmoryn three hundred years ago, all bodies were cremated.

"Thank you."

"You're welcome. I'll have Malwynn and Umaryn help with your mother's body. In the meantime, head over to Jalen and Naomi's over there, and let them know what's happened. They'll take care of you until your father returns."

"Thank you Catherine. My mother would thank you as well," Nick said softly, taking his little sister under his arm.

"With any luck I'll cross paths with her spirit, and she can thank me herself. I'm glad you made it here in time."

Nickolas could only nod. The thought of not making it to the Apostle in time was too much to contemplate.

A gentle gust of wind blew across the crest of the rolling hill just a few miles north of the village of New Picknell. The slender blades of bright green grass waved to and fro, tossed whimsically in the sweet air of the Elmoryn summer.

Summer here in northern Varrland came late, and lasted only a precious couple months. The tiny shoots of grass grew quickly and robustly, living their simply lives to the fullest until the cold and snow came for the long winter that would surely bury them, cutting them off from the life giving sun they grew tall to touch.

The next day Catherine's eldest children walked side by side. The brother and sister strode slowly beside each other under the late season's sun. The brother stood only an inch taller than his sister, and both walked proudly with raven black hair. Slung over his wiry shoulder was a bow that had seen ample use over the past decade. A simple bow, one made to learn and hunt easy prey with, the bow was present more for comfort than for purpose. The quiver at his hip held only a handful of arrows. The sister, lean and strong walked with no weapons. Her bright blue eyes, the same as her sibling's searched the expansive green fields in every direction, looking for something interesting to break the monotony of a quiet day that youth never seemed to find the ability to appreciate fully. The prior day's excitement had already been forgotten.

"How's the forge been?" Malwynn asked his sister. It was the first thing either of the two had said since leaving their small town. Comfortable silence was their way.

"Hot. It's quite the job. I am very excited for when Luther teaches me more advanced techniques soon. I think I'm just as excited for when the colder weather sets in. It'll make the forge considerably more comfortable," the sister replied.

Malwynn looked to his sister Umaryn and smiled proudly. Much like their mother, she was blessed with a rare ability, and had taken a different route than most of the woman in his village, as well as the majority of women across their country of Varrland. Umaryn was spirit touched.

The world of Elmoryn was bursting at the seams with life and energy. Some gifted individuals were blessed with the gift of being able to hear and reach out to the spirits of the dead, gaining insight and power, channeling the very souls of the ancestors into mystical power. Others touched by the spirits were able to connect their own essence to the things that men and women had created. Across Elmoryn all crafted items, especially those of particular quality contained a smidge of spiritual energy, and Umaryn could speak to those spirits, and channel the energy inside into her own mystical talents.

People more experienced with these mystical energies called them The Way. It was said those with the gift to manipulate the many different energies of Elmoryn were said to know The Way. Umaryn was developing her skills with the spirits of the things made by man working in the forge, and eschewing the traditional roles a girl of their age took. She'd make no bread for the man that captured her heart, but she might fashion him a blade of tempered steel that would sing a song that could show him her love.

Malwynn had developed no such talent in The Way. He had managed to become a decent shot with the simple bow hanging on his shoulder, and had earned his father's respect by working hard in the family fields. Malwynn and Umaryn's family was small and tightly knit together. Their mother and father had traveled widely across Varrland and neighboring Duulan for many years, and their experiences had left them yearning for a quiet, safe place to raise their family. New Picknell had sufficed.

Ellioth, the patriarch of the family was a retired scholar, and veteran adventurer. Ellioth had notable skill in wielding a blade and wearing armor, and coupled with his passionate love for discovery he'd made a good living searching out treasures lost in the various wildernesses across Elmoryn. Ellioth was one of the few still living souls that had traveled deep into the Eastern Wilds far to the south. That savage, wild region was known the world over as a one way adventure, filled with death, failure, and sorrow. Ellioth had escaped the monsters and natural threats of the Eastern Wilds with tales that would turn the halest man pale white.

Catherine, mother of Malwynn and Umaryn had met

Ellioth at the Cathedral in Daris where she had worked and lived. The central home of the Church of Souls in Varrland, the Cathedral of Kincaid was a massive nexus of religious energy and population. Catherine was an Apostle, a reasonably skilled user of The Way, and servant of the spirits of the ancestors that roamed Elmoryn. After meeting Ellioth, falling deeply in love, and becoming pregnant with the twins, the couple moved to New Picknell where Catherine took over as the most senior Apostle at the modest church in town. Catherine attended to the births, deaths, healing the sick and wounded, and most importantly, consecrating the bodies of the dead.

The most sacred of all duties an Apostle can perform is the consecration of the dead. It is so important to the Church of Souls, and the very survival of humanity on Elmoryn that it is the first spell taught to Apostles once their gift and devotion is revealed. Everyone on Elmoryn knew what happened to a body left unconsecrated too long... Malwynn's mind drifted back to how close they had been to tragedy yesterday with Julianne's death. A few minutes more, and the entire village might've been in danger.

"Are the fields ready for harvest?" Umaryn asked idly. In truth she wasn't interested, but she and her twin brother had been sharing these long walks since the two could walk, and this was their way.

"Almost. Another month and a half. You know you could ask me the real question you want to. I don't mind." Malwynn said with a wry smile, reading his sister's mind.

Umaryn's eyes lit up with restrained excitement. "I didn't want to pry. How are you and Marissa doing? Are we ready for the thought of marriage? Will I be Aunt Umaryn soon?"

Malwynn almost blushed, the skin of his thin, pale white cheeks taking on a faint redness. "Ha. You're terribly funny. I can't speak to children in the near future, or your ability to be an Aunt to them, but I can comfortably say that by the harvest, I think I'll go to her family and ask their permission for her hand in marriage."

Umaryn giggled ferociously and took her brother's arm, shaking it happily. "Oh I'm so happy for you two! Just imagine it. Malwynn the husband, Malwynn the father. Mom and Dad will just be overwhelmed with joy. Imagine little Rynne being an Aunt too. She'll beam!"

Rynne was their little sister, just ten winters of age. She shared the same midnight black hair and blue eyes as the twins. In just a few more years, she'd be the target of every teenage boy suitor in New Picknell.

"I'm sure she'll be just smitten with the idea of being an aunt. However... I need to find the courage you seem to have in abundance, and find the nerve to ask her parents for her hand first. I'm sure I'll manage. Try not to tell mom and dad though. I'm still waiting a bit longer."

Umaryn beamed, "Not a problem. I'm happy you've trusted me with this little secret. It makes me feel very special." The last bit was delivered with thick sarcasm.

"Mmhm. I'm sure you feel like the most important person in the worl-" Malwynn stopped mid word, looking over the crest of a hill a half minute's jog ahead. "Did you hear that?" The tall, young man's eyed narrowed as he scanned the hill ahead.

Umaryn pointed her eyes at the same spot her brother was investigating, listening intently, trying to sense what he'd sensed. She saw and heard nothing. "I hear nothing. Too much time with the wheat? Not enough time with Marissa has you hearing things eh?"

"I'm telling you, something is happening over that hill. I swear to the ancestors I heard metal on metal. Swords clashing. You're telling me the artificer in the family can't sense two forged items making noise nearby? Come. I want to see what's ahead."

Umaryn's eyes narrowed at Malwynn's stinging insult, but she followed him as he took off running towards his goal. Sometimes he was infuriating.

But brothers can be that way.

Umaryn, always the faster and stronger of the siblings pulled ahead as they ran, cresting the hill and seeing the other side many seconds before her thinner, weaker brother. As she slowed her gait and took in the spectacle before her, the fresh summer air in her lungs turned stale. The coppery stench of raw spilled blood turned her belly sour.

Malwynn reached the peak of the grassy green slope and immediately put his hands on his knees, oblivious to the smell of blood and clamor below. A rapid trio of heavy puffs refilled his empty lungs, and he stood fully, immediately matching his sister's awestruck expression.

War had come to New Picknell.

Evidence showed the battle had only just begun; there were but a few slain bodies on the ground. One man was freshly murdered. His was clad in sturdy leather armor and wore a white and red tunic over it. He had been attacked at the face and neck, and his armor had failed him. His lifeblood was spilled across a swath of the grass in long jets. His arteries had ejected his blood forcefully. His death had been savage, but quick. Two other bodies wore the unmistakable purple collars of the Amaranth Empire to the far north. The dark purple indicated that the defeated were undead in the control of one of the Queen's Necromancers. If there were two destroyed undead nearby...

The necromancer was adorned in a rich purple robe that told of his importance in his home nation. In Amaranth the color purple could only be worn by those in service to the Queen, to wear it without her consent was a death sentence. Under the dark folds of rich cloth he was covered from head to toe in what appeared to be plates of thick carved bone. He wore it like a massive petrified insect might wear their shell.

AT LEAST HE'S NOT ON FIRE

He wielded a wicked looking mace in his left hand, heavy and threatening in its blunt power. His true weapon was his bare right hand. The touch of a necromancer often carried the brutal necrotic power of their dark magic. The necromancer himself was mounted on a Gvorn. Gvorn were rare here in the rural areas of New Picknell. They were natural to the far north, and were massive war and pack beasts. Each Gvorn stood as tall as a war horse, but had a powerful set of horns that mimicked a ram. They had thick wool as well that protected them from the snow, ice, and frigid winds. The Gvorn the purple robed necromancer rode was grey like the winter sky, and had a thick coat of wool. This mount had brought him here from deep in the Amaranth Empire. Possibly from as far as the capital necropolis of Graben.

The necromancer was engaged in mortal combat with a man mounted on a Gvorn that dwarfed his. This rugged beast was a full hand higher than the necromancer's and had been shorn of most of its heavy coat, revealing the dark grey skin beneath. Only a Gvorn from the south would be shaved that way. The man held a rugged shield with the crest of Varrland, and wore dark white and crimson robes over a suit of chain and plate mail. He wore no helm, and his long salt and pepper hair was tied back in a ponytail. It tossed violently about as he swung a gleaming steel long sword at the death mage on the opposing Gvorn. The blade bit into the shoulder of the wizard, cutting a chunk of the bone plate away, and tossing his body nearly out of the saddle.

"Arrgh!" He spat at the knight.

"Invader scum! I'll send you back to your bitch Queen in an urn!" The knight's breath was strong. He was barely breaking a sweat in the battle.

At the feet of his massive mount were the rest of the two opposing forces. Things were precarious for the Varrland forces. They were clearly outmatched in numbers. Still standing and violent were a full half score of undead. Their skin was pale grey, the rotting arrested by foul Amaranth magic. They lashed out at half a dozen men similar to the man missing his throat. They slashed out with short swords and decimating fingers that terminated in ragged yellow fingernails. Fortunately the undead were mindless automatons, attacking with only the barest of skill and instinct.

The worst situation was a trio engaged in battle a few horse lengths past the necromancer and knight. Malwynn and Umaryn clutched hands nervously at the crest of the hill as they watched the fatal dance play out. Two men wearing light armor, heavy cloaks edged in a purple fringe, wielding long and wickedly curved battle axes circled a younger man separated from his group. He could be only a few years older than the twins; no more than three winters, maybe four. He had short dark hair, shaved to only the thickness of the razor that cut it. Like the knight riding the Gvorn still battling with the necromancer he wore heavier armor; chain mixed with plate. Instead of the long sword the knight clearly was expert with, the younger man used a warhammer. It was long, almost the length of a grown man's leg, and had a wicked spike opposite a heavy, hardened steel head. Umaryn admired the weapon's elegant simplicity as he spun it in deadly circles, hand to hand. The weapon's balance must have been near-perfect.

Unfortunately, the martial display was just that; all for show, and not for purpose. The young warrior was simply buying time until help could arrive. The two axe wielding assailants quickly had him turned sideways and flanked as he spun his weapon. Finally, after several long, agonizing seconds, the solitary warrior made his move. He looked to one of the two purple cloaked men and suddenly brought the head of his hammer up lightning fast at the other. His eyes bought him hesitation from the man he struck in the face, but he twisted just a few inches too far, and gave his back up for just a few seconds too long. As the Amaranth soldier fell to the grass with his face broken apart by the hammer his cohort struck the Varrland warrior. The foot long smile of the axe slashed down powerfully at the simple chain right beside the red and white clad warrior's kidneys. Despite the rings of forged steel, the incredible force of the impact ruptured the flesh beneath, sending the man to his knees.

Malwynn's mind suddenly unfroze, and he slipped his bow from his shoulder as the Amaranth warrior raised his axe for the killing blow. Umaryn watched her brother slip an arrow free from his quiver and let it fly. Spinning like a dervish the arrow flew true, past the knight's mount only an inch from the creature's heavy wool coat, and directly into the shoulder of the cloaked invader. The man's hand reflexively gave way as his downward axe stroke fell harmlessly to the side. He looked savagely towards the twins, his glance threatening them. As Malwynn drew another arrow the Amaranth warrior resorted to a weapon that was still effective: his boots. He kicked the wounded warrior in the back of the skull and flattened his body in the blood stained grass. The warrior lay still as the Amaranth soldier with the arrow lodged in his shoulder came running across the melee at the twins. They had only a few seconds before he'd be up the slope and upon them.

The purple robed necromancer shrieked in joy as the warrior fell, taking his eyes off the knight almost as if a powerful narcotic was taking over his mind. As they watched the murderous Amaranth soldier charge their position the knight capitalized on the necromancer's exultation. His Gvorn spun round at his command, putting his sword hand a foot closer to the foreign death mage, and he lunged forward, piercing the bone armor under the cloak in a weak location. The smooth blade penetrated the morbid bone armor with a strong thrust, and the necromancer's high was quickly brought down to earth. He looked over from the fallen Varrlander man to the knight who urged his Gvorn forward, plunging the blade even further in. The necromancer coughed a thick wad of dark blood, and the knight yanked his sword free. His arm cocked back, and he sent a mailed fist into the jaw of the evil wizard, knocking him off the ghostly grey Gvorn. Umaryn and Malwynn watched as the necromancer's neck twisted disturbingly to the side as he crunched into the ground. His body settled in a manner that planted his dead face into the grass. As his body shuddered the remainder of life inside it, and his throat released the final breath ever taken in, the armor that encased his body suddenly faded from reality. In death, the necromancer's magic faded.

Their attention switched back to the man almost upon them. Malwynn had another arrow ready and was drawing the string to launch it as the man hefted his axe upwards with his good arm. Umaryn, ever the clever one, stepped instinctively to the side of the man, flanking him almost exactly as the two Amaranth warriors had flanked the Varrlander. Malwynn's fingers opened, and the arrow bolted off into the chest of their attacker, piercing the chainmail. The arrow didn't go far though, the chain was of good quality, and Mal had not drawn the string fully. Nonetheless the arrow staggered the rage faced man, and Umaryn struck. She had produced a small hammer from somewhere, Malwynn didn't know from where, nor did he care. She snarled and sent the hammer at the rear of the man's head with a backhanded stroke. The forge tool crunched into the base of his skull and Malwynn watched the man's eyes roll to the whites instantly. He fell down at their feet and twitched several times as the life left his body.

"Finish them!" The knight hollered in his confident baritone. The remaining Varrlander foot soldiers had managed to quell the undead threat with their superior blades and dexterity. The undead were a powerful threat to the common folk, but to armed and armored soldiers, it would take many of the animated dead to be a true threat. Many, or more powerful kinds. As the last undead had its head separated from its body the knight brought his massive war beast over to the twins, clearly surprised at their presence. He had already cleaned and sheathed his blade, and with a silk cloth in his free hand he was wiping away the spatters of fresh Amaranth blood from his face. He stopped his mount a few paces from the panting, adrenaline crashing twins.

"What brought you two out to such a remote place today? If it weren't for your participation against the Queen's insurgents I'd suggest you were their allies. Are you locals?" He asked, his tone somewhat thankful.

Umaryn answered. She was calmer than her brother, "Yes... We are from New Picknell, several miles to the south east of here. We'd had a challenging day and wanted a quiet walk."

The knight smiled, "Not what you expected."

The twins shook their heads, taking in the carnage and devastation the fight had unleashed. It was as if a bloody sore had appeared out of the ether, and spewed forth dead bodies, and sadness.

"Boy, what is your name? You've some skill with that bow."

Malwynn was lost in his thoughts and frayed emotions, but gathered himself, "I am Malwynn sir. And I've little skill with this bow. An ancestor guided my actions, no doubt. This is my twin sister Umaryn."

"Greetings to you both Malwynn and Umaryn. Your family resemblance is quite strong. My name is Knight Captain Marcus Gray," the knight said with a smile before continuing. "The dead only assist those worthy of helping Malwynn. Your skill is not to be left out of the equation son. I thank you for joining the fight against the Amaranthines here. You nearly saved Chael's life. I'm sad to see an Apostle go. Do you know where there might be another Apostle? Is there one by chance in New Picknell?"

The two siblings were floored. They'd watched an Apostle die. Malwynn was the first to speak, "Our mother is an Apostle. Chael was his name? We didn't know he was an Apostle. I'm... I'm sorry we didn't save him. I wish I'd drawn my bow a moment earlier."

The knight dismissed his apology with a sad shake of his head, "He was a warrior too, and when you take your faith to the front lines, you may die for it. He knew the risk and continued forth. He was a good man and died a good death. But now we must ensure that he does not become what he hated so. Can you show us to your mother? We have dead to attend to, and she seems to be our source for the Blessing of Soul's rest."

Umaryn and Malwynn nodded simultaneously, as they often did. Together, the Varrlanders gathered up the bodies that needed their souls set free, and they set off back to New Picknell.

Quiet, and safe New Picknell.

- Chapter Two -
Normalcy Shattered

"We live in complicated times," Marcus Gray said quietly the next morning. Around the long wooden table worn smooth by a decade of plates, silverware and elbows sat Malwynn and Umaryn's entire family, as well as the large warrior. Even out of his heavy armor he was wide and tall. His hair wasn't in the ponytail as it was the previous day during the battle; it had been let down and hung around the top of his shoulders.

Little Rynne sat in her elder sister's lap. She was absolutely smitten with the guest, and the best seat was Umaryn's lap. Umaryn sat directly beside the hulking warrior from the south, and Rynne leaned over her older sister's arm, her eyes locked onto the relaxed warrior.

Elliott, the father of the family nodded to affirm Marcus' statement, "Things are never simple children. Your mother and I have traveled much of this world, and discovered many things, but no matter what you learn, there is always more to find. Always one more stone to turn over."

"Why are times complicated?" Umaryn asked Marcus simply.

The Varrlander knight finished chewing his modest bite of eggs before replying, "Umaryn, to our north is a nation that has been ruled over by an unbroken line of Queens for two centuries. From each mother to her daughter the line hasn't been broken once, and the Purple Throne has controlled that nation with an iron fist. In the Empire you pay fealty to the Queen or you serve her in death."

"You could choose to leave. You could choose to fight her," Malwynn offered hopefully.

Marcus shook his head slowly, "There is no choice. Graben is too far to walk, and any mounted locals trying to leave would almost certainly be caught by the Queen's militia, or ancestors forbid, her personal Order."

"Order?" Rynne asked in her innocent child's voice.

"The Order of the Purple Flower. A hundred gvorn mounted elite warriors that answer to the Queen alone. They have a legion of undead in the wings for their military actions as well. Many of their numbers are necromancers as well. Necromancers of a much higher caliber than the simpleton my people faced down yesterday. He was of marginal skill, clearly."

"Wow," Rynne answered, only barely comprehending the full weight of the man's answer to her.

"Things are made complicated by the Empire's greed for territory. Things are made complicated by the Empire's need for dead bodies to perform slave labor. Things are made complicated by their constant incursions into Varrland to satisfy these hungers. Things are made complicated by our own Varrlander pride, and sense of patriotism and independence. Don't forget, we are only a few generations removed from the execution of our own tyrant king. Our national blood boils when we see a nation so close under so similar a rule. It also does help that our envoys to the Realm of Duulan have not yet met with the Queen to make peace."

Catherine leaned in and addressed the knight, "How would that help things? You think a Duulani diplomat will achieve what a Varrlander diplomat can't?"

Marcus nodded confidently, "For whatever reason the current Queen of Amaranth is fond of the King of Duulan. She has listened to his advice many times in the past decade, averting many a crisis, and we are petitioning the King to send missives and diplomats to her to stop this reckless activity. If she does not..." Marcus trailed off, fidgeting with the remnants of food on his plate.

"If she doesn't what then?"

Marcus looked up with cold eyes, devoid of joy, "Then Varrland would be forced to escalate matters."

Malwynn felt the mood of the room drop as if snow had

fallen fresh and piled a foot high, "You mean war. You mean Varrland might go to war with the Empire."

"I mean that is a distinct possibility. The Empire has never sent a force this far into Varrland. It speaks of brazen aggression to send a patrol such as the one you and your sister witnessed yesterday so far into our country. It is a strong sign of things likely to come. Unless deterred by force or diplomacy, I can see no other end to this madness."

"Surely the King of Duulan will send assistance. He must understand the urgency of the matter. War between nations hasn't occurred in centuries. The potential for massacre without the presence of hundreds of Apostles… It could be as bad or worse than The Great Plague. All of humanity would be at risk once more…" Catherine said, worry thick in her voice. Poor little Rynne absorbed the tension and got out of Umaryn's lap, and scurried around to her mother, seeking the best shelter from the unknown.

"Agreed," Marcus said. "It is made more cumbersome by the presence of so many death mages in the Empire. Surely they would use The Way to animate their dead as well as ours. We would be fighting two wars simultaneously."

"What of the Waymancers in The Northern Protectorate at the school of The Way? They'd intervene, wouldn't they?" Umaryn asked.

Marcus shook his head negatively, "House Kulare's presence has been the sole reason the Empire hasn't attempted to invade the NP. If House Kulare came to our aid, the Queen would surely strike at them. The Protectorate's quarries and natural resources are far too enviable for her to simply leave alone. The Waymancers there are focused on keeping their home safe, and teaching the new users of The Way properly. To ask them to do more would be selfish, and reckless."

"What of the other major Knightly Orders?" Ellioth asked, rubbing his hand softly on his youngest child's back. Rynne's emotions had reined themselves in with her mother and father's comforting touch.

Marcus finally nodded, indicating hope, "It is likely that we could receive aid from The Order of the Flame. They have no love lost for the Purple Queen. However, they could spare few knights. They've sworn an oath to the nation of Farmington and would not leave them fully, even for such a just cause. The Order of the Lacuna would certainly send warriors to our aid, but they are spread very thin. If it were to come to war, Varrland would need to carry the day expecting no help. We would need to start and finish any war on our own, or at least expect to. Let us hope that this does not come to war, and the Purple Queen hears reason from the lips of the Duulani King."

The family was in agreement.

"Your hospitality has been enormous. I and my men are in your debt for many reasons this morning," Marcus said, pulling his hair up into the ponytail he wore the other day.

"It's been our pleasure to host you. I'm sure our neighbors looking after your men would say the same. We don't get many visitors to new Picknell, never mind a knight from Daris that's just fought off an Empire patrol." Ellioth said with a smile.

"Nevertheless, we are in your debt. Please don't let my warmongering affect your sleep. I am a leader of men that may be forced to war. Conflict clouds my thoughts."

Catherine's warm face looked to him, "If you wish it, I'll spend some time with you and your men privately. A few blessings from the ancestors for your journey back to Daris might help clear your thoughts, and recover your spent courage."

Marcus admired the mother, and Apostle. "Of course. My men would certainly appreciate your attention. My sincere thanks for all you've done. I'm going to collect my men and return here in a few hours. As a gesture of faith I would like to leave a few gifts behind, if you allow it."

Malwynn and Umaryn perked up at the idea of gifts. Things new to their small town were rare and wondrous items, no matter how trivial. Ellioth's facial expression indicated to Marcus that he should continue.

"I see your elder daughter works with her hands. Her deft use of a forging hammer helped save her brother's life. With even a remote chance of threat on the horizon, I would like to give to her my Apostle Chael's warhammer. I suspect her natural gifts might allow her to make excellent use of it. I know Chael would approve."

Umaryn's eyes lit up like she'd been struck by a bolt of lightning from a storm head, "You're serious?"

"Of course I am. You and your brother risked much trying to save his life, and I feel it appropriate that you take his weapon, and give it a purpose."

"Ancestors bless you, thank you so much," Umaryn said, clearly grateful to the large man.

"I would also like to leave something for your eldest son Ellioth. A gift that may outshine the simple warhammer today."

Malwynn looked around the room, waiting anxiously to hear what could possibly be more incredible than the weapon his sister had received.

"I wish to leave the Gvorn mount the death mage rode with Malwynn. I feel it will be put to much better use in your fields than underneath another warrior, good or evil. Sometimes it is important that a warrior retire gracefully, and I feel this Gvorn's time has come."

The family let loose a series of gasps. Gvorn were incredibly expensive, and owned only by the wealthy, or warriors who required the powerful creatures to do battle. Having one as a farm creature would be an incredible boon not only to Malwynn and the family, but to the whole village.

"I don't even have words to express my appreciation Sir Marcus. This gift seems like too much," Malwynn said softly.

"I thought you would say as much, and I disagree. Rename it. Give it a new purpose, and a new life that isn't dedicated to the ruination of man. I will consider it a task appointed to you."

Malwynn nodded solemnly.

"I will be leaving the rest of the armor and weapons from the Amaranth warriors in your care Ellioth, should you need to arm your citizens more robustly at a later date. I trust you can handle this task?" Marcus asked seriously.

The father nodded, "Of course."

"Then I am off to gather my men. Thank you for the breakfast, and I will see you again before we depart." Marcus stood to his full height and excused himself from the modest dining room. He looked like a shining gem dressed in his finery in the simple home. The family was too excited to say anything for some time.

In the center of the town where the largest well was, Catherine summoned the attention of the ancestors once more to give Marcus and his men a blessing. The entire population of New Picknell, all 167 souls had gathered to watch their departure. Each of the red and white garbed men took her gentle touch on their forehead as if it were a draught of cooling water on the hottest of midsummer days. They felt invigorated, and made more substantial with the support of the spirits in the world around them. To a one, they felt truly and completely blessed by Catherine and the spiritual energy she channeled into them.

Marcus shook many hands before pulling his large body up into the saddle on the back of his massive Gvorn. Taking the reins in hand, he waved and smiled at every person gathered, sharing his tremendous charisma and personal strength. The man seemed to radiate confidence and calm. Malywnn and Umaryn stood next to one another as they waved him goodbye. Umaryn cradled Chael's warhammer in the crook of her arm like a royal scepter, comforted in a way that only the Artificer spirit-touched could be by its presence. They watched for some time as the small group of warriors moved off into the distance, and over a gentle rolling hill.

The brother and sister would have many dark days before they laid eyes on him again.

Many days later Malwynn rested deep in a pile of hay with the young girl he was in love with, looking up at the tall apex of the barn they hid inside. New Picknell had returned to normal. The two were stealing this moment. Marissa's parents would not approve of so intimate a moment for the two yet, and as young lovers, parental wishes were quite secondary. The hay was old; the dried up leftovers from the prior year, and was mostly straw now. It was itchy against his pale white skin, but the soft scent of flowers wafting up from Marissa's hair was more than enough to distract him from such a minor discomfort. He felt her wiggle her arm playfully under his back so as to fully envelop him in an embrace. Marissa rested her delicate head in the crux of his arm and looked up into his eyes.

"Strange week we've had," she said quietly.

"Yeah, no doubt," Malwynn said, meeting her gaze. He bent down and kissed her affectionately and playfully.

"My father says you were quite lucky. He thinks you and your sister are a little crazy for having done what you did."

Malwynn snickered, "Well we're crazy, that's for sure, but not crazy for that. We were trying to help Varrlander knights. It might seem silly now, but we had no time to think about silliness. Just time enough to act." The tall boy's thoughts raced back to the moment his second arrow pierced the chain mail of the Empire foot soldier. Malwynn had been less than a second away from being hacked apart by the vicious axe that now rested in his father's closet.

Marissa nodded, but she didn't fully understand. There was no way for her to. "I'm glad you and your sister didn't get hurt. There were undead there, plus a necromancer. Any number of horrible things could have happened. I don't know what I'd do if I lost you Malywnn. I think I'd go mad."

"It wouldn't be a far trip dear," Malwynn said, picking on her. She retaliated by freeing her hands and mercilessly tickling him. The young man giggled until he couldn't breathe, finally begging her for mercy. She relented. After catching their wind the two nuzzled against one another again, sinking deep into the itchy hay and not caring in the least.

"You know I'm serious. I do think I'd go quite mad if anything happened to you," Marissa said again, seriously.

Malwynn reached down with a free hand and tilted her face up with a finger on her tiny chin, "Marissa, nothing will ever happen to me like that. And I know you love me, and I love you too. I love you more than I'll ever really be able to explain, or understand. Nothing will change that, and from now on, I will do my best to stay safe so you don't have to worry."

Marissa smiled at him, this time fully understanding him, and they kissed softly, this time longer.

"I'd go a little mad myself if anything happened to you. You know that right?"

"Well THAT would be a short trip, wouldn't it?" Marissa said before biting Malwynn's arm with a grin.

Furious tickling ensued.

Umaryn's face was soaked in sweat. Long black tendrils

AT LEAST HE'S NOT ON FIRE

of her hair clung to the moisture on her forehead and neck, absorbing the salty liquid her pores pushed out. Her muscles burned. Every knot and cord of tendon, sinew, and ligament from the tips of her toes to the top of head ached at least a little. The slender but steely woman raised a hand clad in a thick leather glove holding a torn slip of fabric to her face. She swiped it along her brow, then her nose and cheeks, taking away the salty sweat that threatened to drown her.

"Make sure you drink water girl. There are no heroes in the forge," Luther, Umaryn's mentor said. He was a short man, barely reaching Umaryn's shoulder, but he was built like a draft horse, or a Gvorn. Umaryn often joked with the shaven headed man that even his finger and toe nails had muscles. She wasn't entirely sure whether or not they actually were muscled.

The black haired woman nodded, unable to respond with voice. She tossed the rag over her shoulder and walked over to the wooden pail the two smiths drank from. After fetching two ladles of cool water, one for her face, one for her mouth and dry throat, she finally regained her voice, "Luther how do you know there are no heroes in the forge? What of the grand creators that manage to make Artifacts? Aren't they just a little bit of a hero?"

"Touché little one. I suppose they are indeed heroes in many people's eyes. If you get right down to it, I often feel that you are my hero. On more than one occasion in fact." Luther grunted, shuffling items about and getting ready for their next project.

"I'm your hero? You must be joking."

"Not in the least. I'm simply a smith, you see. I heat raw, crude iron, and I hammer it into usable shapes. Not a minor task, I grant. But the iron doesn't speak to me like it does to you. I'm not spirit touched like you are. I can't hear what the iron wants to be. I force it to my will only by brute strength. You work with the iron like it is your friend, and when your skill matches your natural gift, what you will be able to create will be my envy darling. It is a thing of beauty to watch even your novice hands work. "

Umaryn blushed powerfully in the heat of the forge, "I don't know what to say."

"Say you will harness your gift. And tell me you'll get the hell back to work. Arrogant kid. You get one damn compliment and just stop working entirely. Your generation makes me sick," Luther said, turning away to hide the smile on his face.

Umaryn grinned ear to ear and fetched another ladle of water to slake her powerful thirst. As she tipped the drink up and let the cool water fill her mouth she looked over to the wall where her new warhammer leaned. In the recesses of her mind and soul she could almost hear the pure voice of the hammer, and wondered where it had been made, and who had struck the shape of it. It was a fantastic weapon, and she burned to match its creator's talent. More so than ever, she wanted to put hammer to iron, and to listen to the sounds of the spirits being born underneath her strikes.

As the days wore on in New Picknell life settled back in to the normal grind. Malwynn's life became easier as he learned to use the massive Gvorn left to him by Marcus. He chose the name Bramwell for it, and decided that he would let its coat grow out a bit as the summer came to an end. His thick coat would be a boon come winter. Bramwell was a tremendous gift to the family, allowing for Malwynn to move heavy cart loads about town much faster, as well as for riding, and general labor. He made a decision to save all his Varrland marks so he could take a train trip south to Daris to buy a saddle that was fitting for the creature. The necromancer's saddle had a strange air about it that made Malwynn feel queasy. He kept it in the barn with the

AT LEAST HE'S NOT ON FIRE

family's two horses. The two family horses Tinder and Sky were put into quite a fervor when Bramwell first joined them, but after a full week, they were comfortable with the larger creature's presence.

Umaryn's hard work in the forge continued. Luther never mentioned any envy of her again, but Umaryn often wondered just how much potential she had for him to say such a thing. Luther was a modest man that spent little time complimenting anyone, or anything. If she did something perfect, he simply said, "good." Anything less than good was met with a tirade about a lack of work ethic, and how she was wasting his time. She still loved him like a second father though, and despite her frustration with his ways, he was a wonderful teacher for her to apprentice under. She had already learned much, and she knew in the years to come she'd learn far more.

Malwynn spoke to his mother and father about Marissa as well. Ellioth and Catherine were smitten nearly as much by the pretty girl that lived down the way, and when Malwynn spoke to them seriously and full of trepidation about marrying her, their hearts swelled with pride and love. To watch their son fall in love, and reach the point of truly joyous marriage was beyond heartwarming for the two of them. Ellioth agreed it was a wonderful idea, and Catherine the same. The mother also said she would be delighted to look over the ceremony if Marissa and Marissa's family said yes. Malwynn vowed that he'd speak to her parents in a day or two, and the family concocted a grand scheme to get her out of the home so he could do just that.

Early at dawn the next day both Malwynn and Umaryn were sitting at the same well worn table they'd shared since their early childhood. The familiar smell of Catherine's hands, and Ellioth's pipe smoke were worn into the wood more permanently than any stain could be. Malwynn traced faint lines where he'd pressed his fingernails into the wood as a child when forced to eat the vegetables he'd hated so. Now he ate them with relish, and laughed at the tiny gouges he'd left so long ago. Now there were tiny fingernail marks in the table from their little sister Rynne for similar reasons. Umaryn sipped on a thick mug of hot coffee she'd poured from a glass press a few minutes prior. The dark rich liquid steamed into the cool summer morning air and Malwynn savored the scent. He had no taste for the brew, but the scent tickled memories, and that he loved very much. Umaryn let the dark drink cascade warmly to her stomach and invigorate her mind.

"I think we should take Bramwell out for a ride. Maybe to the north hills? Check on the blueberries and pick some to make pies later? Or maybe we can talk mom into making her special cobbler? What do you think?" Malwynn offered the idea to his sister. Jaunts like these were common for them, though never before with a Gvorn.

"Your large friend would make gathering a few buckets of berries a lot easier," Umaryn said between sips of coffee.

"Yeah. We could also pack a small lunch, and eat out there. I think mom was going to spend some time over at the Reegan house helping old man Reegan with his arthritis. She'll be tied up over there for hours. He's like a magnet, you just can't get away from him once he gets started telling stories about the great undead outbreak in his home town as a kid. Remember when we used to go out there with dad? He'd pretend to be an Ice Bear, and we'd pretend to be rangers from the Great Land Shelf? Oh ancestors, we were silly. It was so much fun though." Malwynn watched the steam rise off of his sister's mug wistfully. He was reminiscing a lot lately as he mulled over the marriage proposal. It felt to him like his whole world was about to change. He couldn't be more correct.

Umaryn smiled with him. "Let me finish my coffee. If you get Bramwell ready, I'll grab Tinder."

"Deal." Malwynn stood up on legs still creaky from sleep, and headed back to his room to gather his things for a morning out. It would be glorious to ride Bramwell as his sister rode Tinder with the sun warming the day.

AT LEAST HE'S NOT ON FIRE

Umaryn savored her hot drink.

When the twins were small children Ellioth would take them out to the north hills outside New Picknell. The land was the last bump in the earth before becoming flat and heading further north into the steadily cooling territory of the Empire. Despite seeming very far away, in truth, the lands of the Purple Queen were frighteningly close.

On their tiny legs with their father leading them it would take Umaryn and Malwynn almost two solid hours of walking to reach the dark green hills covered in low lying blueberries. They'd arrive each time covered in the innocent sweat a hot child often is, with their father beckoning them to take a drink of water from his skin before they gorged themselves sick on the plump blue gems they'd walked so far to pick. Of course one or both of them would stick too many of the berries into their bellies, and they'd pay the price by sending them back up forcefully with their father shaking his head and laughing all the while. The lessons learned by youth.

This time the twins had far more patience, and on the gentle backs of Bramwell and Tinder the journey took only half an hour. Also, they were here not only to pluck the fruits, but to simply spend a little bit of time together. In truth, both knew that in a day or two their lives could and would change. No one expected Marissa's parents to rebuke Malwynn, son of the town's lone Apostle and most learned sage. Uniting their daughter with him was not only the right thing to do for the young couple, but also a smart move for their family. It would be a move up in status for them in the town, and it would bring the two families together. Consumed by her thoughts, Umaryn debated all the different paths their lives could take in just a few days.

Umaryn would finally have a bedroom to her own in the family home. No longer would she have to share a bed with little Rynne. Both thoughts pained her. She'd miss her brother's presence fiercely, but she lamented the thought of not comforting her smaller sister each night as she drifted off into sleep. The dark haired apprentice of the forge wondered how little Rynne would take to sleeping alone. Umaryn would also see her brother far less as he set out and made his own home. Knowing Malwynn's work ethic he would set out and lay fence at the edge of town near the family farm and claim it as his own. He'd take the Gvorn and ready the land for crops, and within a year his hard work would pay off with green gardens, and food to eat and sell. It was likely that before a single bite of food reached the table Marissa would be a mother. Umaryn wasn't a fool, and knew the two of them were already making love. She envied the intimacy her brother had found with another, but she knew it wasn't her time yet. Umaryn was focused on, no- she was obsessed with learning more about her craft. A man would come some day that would win her heart, give her another thing to obsess over and until then, she swallowed her envy away and replaced it with joy for her brother's future. Soon she'd share a future like his.

She would of course throw herself into the work at the forge. Her life as a smith would probably flourish. No distractions like these jaunts to the countryside for berries to get in the way of her practice with Luther. All that extra time with the barrel shaped man would lead to many new skills, and hours and hours of back breaking work. As she watched Malwynn pluck sun ripened berries from dark leaved bushes she wondered how much muscle she'd put on, and whether or not it would be attractive to a man. She shrugged and went back to pulling berries like her brother.

Umaryn half kneeled to reach the fruit. Hers was a better way than his. Inside he laughed, wishing he could gather the berries with his bow somehow. The tall young man looked to the sky and over to the horizon where the ghostly faint image of the cool moon Lune could be seen. Lune's grayish blue orb was slung just above the green grass of the hills and looked so much larger than it usually did. Malwynn wondered how long it'd be before Hestia, Lune's smaller red sister moon appeared trailing behind it. Malwynn's eyes registered something in the foreground, and they shifted their focus slowly, bringing it into reality. Snaking across the top of the sky above his head there was a thin, gray black smudge. Malwynn tipped his head up until he stared straight up into the sky, then a little further, and then a bit more, following the smudge back to its source over a hill they crossed to get to the blueberry patch. Malwynn had his head in the thick low lying blueberries before he realized where his eyes were pointed. He rolled over, bringing the world right-side-up, and as he was struck with horrible dread, he felt his pulse quicken.

"Umaryn," he said apprehensively, voice full of worry.

"Yeah?" She replied, not looking to where her brother looked, or hearing the emotion underlying his message.

"Look over here. There's smoke in the sky."

Malwynn looked over his shoulder at her and watched as she put two and two together. "You think that's coming from home?"

"It's an awful lot of smoke sis."

Umaryn put her nose to the air and lowered her mental focus on the real world. As a fledgling Artificer she should have little ability to sense what was burning, especially so far away, but it was worth a try. She inhaled deeply, forcing the air fully through her nostrils and far into her belly, giving her senses a chance to filter out what the source of the smoke might be.

Immediately images of hewn wood, plaster, brick and nails flashed into her conscious. She saw wallpaper peeling, toys burning, and furniture ablaze. She caught millisecond views of thick curls of black smoke wafting menacingly out from walls and floors as bright orange tongues of flame belched free, reaching out hungry for more oxygen. The place was familiar to her. It was intimate and permanent in her mind. Umaryn was momentarily paralyzed by the inaudible screams of the spirits of the items in her vision burning, and felt their remote destruction more fully in an instant than she'd felt any physical pain in her whole life. By the time the visions passed only a second had elapsed, and her eyes were already full to the brim with thick tears, and every nerve ending in her tense body was electrified with stimulation. Malwynn watched as she reeled. Once she gained her balance Umaryn coughed, retched a dry heave, and looked to him desperately.

"Our house is burning."

The two scrambled to their feet. They had to get home immediately.

Flames ate at every wooden surface in New Picknell with ferocity. It burned with a ferocity born of The Way, not of merely just nature. No fire could burn as hot, or spread as fast without pure magic fueling its movement and power. By the time Tinder and Bramwell carried the brother and sister back to where they'd grown up, the only thing remaining in the village was blackened frames of homes, and brick chimneys. Bodies torched in the intense heat were drawn tight by burnt skin and flesh, or split open by blades and charred. In the fields the two saw cows, goats and sheep slain by the dozen, their bodies left wastefully in pools of their own blood. Whoever had come to New Picknell came to raze and destroy it, not pillage it for loot.

Both brother and sister were overcome with emotion as they rode around the edge of the town. Unlike many other Elmoryn towns, New Picknell had no city wall. Walls in a world where the dead came back to unlife were practical for many reasons. New Picknell relied on farm fences, and around these the twins rode. The heat of the coals was still too much to persuade the two mounts to go closer, so they rode in circles over and over, watching as the final flames died out, and as the final homes crumbled, leaving nothing but memories and burnt cinders in their wake. One hand of each was wrapped tightly around the reins of their mount while the other hand continuously wiped away tears from eyes burning from smoke in the air. The stench of death was more powerful than either of them could've ever imagined. Malwynn felt that even the ancestors could smell the ruined town and its dead inhabitants from across the veil.

"Everyone is dead. They are all dead," Umaryn said, her throat hoarse from the yelling and screaming she'd just given up on.

Malwynn rested his hands, still clutching Bramwell's reins in his lap. He knew she spoke the truth, "There's a chance someone is alive. Someone had to have escaped this, and whoever did it. Maybe my Marissa survived?"

"No. No one escaped. Marissa is gone Malwynn, I'm sorry. You know as well as I do. We'd have seen them by now," Umaryn said, deflated.

Malwynn had no response. He simply wiped away the tear streaming to his jaw. His life had been shattered.

"Who did this? Who would come to New Picknell and murder it? Who would murder a whole village, and leave?" Umaryn asked. Her mind was dangerously close to unfurling, and spilling apart like a melon dropped from too high.

"Someone trying to prove a point. Someone who didn't like New Picknell interfering in their business."

The dark haired woman sat up straight in Tinder's saddle, her emotions suddenly kindled in a new direction; towards hatred. "You think the Empire is responsible for this? You think those purple fucks rode here and smote our home because of the fight the other day?"

Malwynn was taken aback by his sister's language, "We'll have to see if there are many bodies left. If it was the Empire, I'd imagine they'd take many of the bodies home for their foul mages to resurrect as undead. I know we've seen some dead, but their bodies were ruined by the fire. If many of our townsfolk are missing, I say it points a finger directly at Graben. Straight north to the hands of the Purple Queen."

"I'll find whoever did this. I swear to all the spirits denied today in these deaths. I swear to all the ancestors that have come before us, all the spirits that will come after us, and I swear to every spirit of all things made. I will find who did this, and they will rue the day they came to my home, and did this." Umaryn said, her voice full of hardened steel, and freshly tempered hatred.

Malwynn felt the hair on the back of his neck stand as he listened to the strength of her statement, "I will be there every step of the way with you. You will not shed a drop of blood without my presence to catch it. The death of our family, and my love will not go unanswered."

Oaths given, the two sat silently, watching their village collapse into ash forever.

Malwynn used an arm long length of hewn timber to lift and move debris off a dead body, grimacing as he saw and recognized the face. He called out to his sister, "It's old man Reegan. He's been split up the middle with a blade. Something big. Dead long before the fire ever touched his flesh." Malwynn moved his piece of wood, flipping the debris up and off of the old man's corpse. He tossed his stick aside towards Bramwell and took one of old man Reegan's legs to drag him to a central spot where the twins had been collecting the bodies. There were very few bodies. Only thirty and they'd searched most of the town already.

Umaryn's face was covered in streaks of black. She'd been elbow deep in soot covered drudgery since they had been able to come inside the town. It was only a few hours from sunset, and they'd yet to find a living survivor. Soon the evening chill would come, along with the winds across the plains. "I think that's it. We can check the foundation basements, but if I had to wager on what we'd find…"

"We'll be finding no one. You were right Umaryn. Everyone is dead."

The two said nothing for several minutes as they looked at the pile of bodies they'd collected. It was far too large, and far too real.

"I think there is enough wood for a proper pyre. Mother had a cord of wood the other day behind the barn. The barn is gone, but the wood… The wood might still be there."

Malwynn nodded slowly. "We will need to collect supplies. We've no money. No food. All our clothes are gone in the fire."

It was Umaryn's turn to nod, "Help me with the wood. These bodies are sure to sit back up soon and seek fresh blood unless we burn them. I'm surprised they haven't sat up and bitten one of us yet. Mother would scold us."

The last sentence hit both brother and sister hard. Mother wouldn't be scolding them for anything anymore.

It turned both of their stomachs to be sitting near a funeral pyre, and to be thankful for its warmth. The sun had indeed set, as it had done every day since time immemorial, and the chill had come as expected. They huddled tight to one another with the single blanket they'd found draped over their shoulders. It was a meager shelter, but they were warmed by the pyre's flames without, and the inner burning desire for vengeance within.

They looked up at the stars and gave each one a name. A name for a resident of New Picknell they knew. A name for a friend they knew. A name for a dead person.

They would not shiver that night.

Umaryn headed to the forge at dawn's first light, her skin still caked with the blackness from the night before. She watched as Hestia, the tiny red moon dipped over the horizon and hid for the remainder of the day. At the ruins of the forge she found no bodies. Luther may have died at the forge, but his body did not stay there. Perhaps, if he was fortunate his flesh and bones were consumed in the flames of the forge, where workers of metal might find peace in the afterlife. She hoped as much as she could he had met that fate, though she suspected something far darker came of his end.

Lying in the dirt of the forge she found all that remained; the heads of hammers, and the warped, twisted wreckage of tools that couldn't withstand the overpowering flames that destroyed the workplace. There was precious little she could salvage, but she took what was still conceivably useful. She took these things less out of hope that they'd be usable, and more for their emotional value. Every piece she walked away with was one more memory salvaged in her mind.

Far away, across the expanse of the flattened village and all alone Malwynn sat cross legged in the middle of the street. He was in front of the void that had been Marissa's home. His eyes had no focus. The bright blue seemed muted now, filled with a grey that came from his tortured soul within. Malwynn's thoughts lacked focus. His emotions roiled to and fro from happiness to sadness. From joy brought on by happy recollections to the unending grief brought on by his reality. He was so unhappy, and had no way to express it.

The only thing left of Marissa's home was the large flat stone that had rested as their doorstep. Nothing else remained. Malwynn looked at and traced his eyes along the cracks caused by the heat of the flames. It had been rough before, but that texture made it safe, like the sure footing you got from sand tossed on ice. Now the stone was melted to a smoother consistency, and crisscrossed with fissures that looked like black veins. He remembered the evening last fall that he and Marissa had shared their first kiss on that stone. He'd brought her home after taking her for their third "date." It was simply a walk around town, taking a few minutes to stop in at the forge to meet Umaryn, and watch her make a horseshoe. Umaryn had approved of Marissa that night, and he'd felt so happy he'd given the pretty girl a nervous kiss on the cheek when he brought her home. Marissa had returned his awkward advance with a retaliatory kiss on the lips before stealing away inside.

So long ago.

Umaryn fell to the ground shortly after Malwynn's mind drifted away. She sat cross legged as he was. "Thirty two bodies. That leaves one hundred thirty five unaccounted for, assuming dad's population count was right. What did you say that would mean?"

Malwynn blinked several times to clear his mind and return to the present, "I thought it meant this was the Empire's deed. They animate their victims and bring them home to put them to work. Like the necromancer Marcus killed. He had undead with him."

"Do you think the Empire did this?" Umaryn asked, dragging the tip of an old pair of pliers in the dirt of the street, drawing the shape of a segment of armor she'd imagined while daydreaming.

"Of course they did. We fought back against their patrol,

so they came and ruined New Picknell. They took our dead, and left us this-, this destruction."

"What do we do? I can't just move on from this brother. I swore an oath to find justice and I will see to it, come Hell or high water."

Malwynn nodded, his eyes fixed on Marissa's doorstep, "There is no hell. Just the ancestor state."

"Mother said the spirits know there's more beyond where they are. Heaven and Hell. And I'm saying Hell won't stop me from smashing the skulls of the people responsible for this apart."

"Whatever," Malwynn said bitterly, avoiding the bulk of the reasonless argument.

"Don't whatever me. We need a plan Mal. Where are we going? What are we going to do? You've always been the smarter one. Dad always made you read."

The compliment caught Malwynn by surprise and he smiled. It was his first smile since seeing black smoke in the sky. He spent a few moments analyzing the potential future ahead of them, and then committed to a plan. "We gather what we can. We head north and west to look for the tracks of who did this. See if they headed into the Empire. If we have to, we head to Graben itself and find out who did this."

"How will we manage that? We've never been anywhere Mal. We'll stick out like a sore thumb in the Empire. We'll never be able to find anyone there without rousing suspicion. We'd get ourselves killed like everyone here."

Malwynn smiled in a way that made Umaryn uneasy. It was predatory, almost wolf-like. "We won't rouse any suspicion if that Amaranth armor Marcus left for us survived the fire. Father locked it away in the basement in his metal chest. If it made it through the fire, we should be able to waltz over the border and straight to Graben. Then, it's a simple matter of carefully inflicting pain on people until we find who did this to our families."

It was Umaryn's turn to smile like a predator.

- Chapter Three -
The Road to Ockham's Fringe

"I hate to say this, but the purple looks good on you," Umaryn said, grudgingly looking at her brother in the Amaranth armor. A stroke of luck had preserved just two sets of the salvaged gear.

"If you hate to say it, then don't say it," Malwynn returned, adjusting the fit of the armor. It made him itchy.

"Yeah yeah yeah," Umaryn said, adjusting the fit of her own armor.

Malwynn looked and took her in. The armor they both wore was primarily made of leather. Umaryn said it was Gvorn leather, but Malwynn couldn't tell. His sister probably whispered to the thick skin and it told her its name. He'd never understand The Way. She was right though. The armor was good looking. The smooth dark brown leather had a rich and earthy tone to it, like the delicious Oakdale chocolate their mother bought from the markets in Daris. Arranged geometrically across the entire leather surface of the armor were steel studs, or rivets, that added extra protection. Many were shiny, almost like chrome in nature, but a sizeable amount were rust colored, stained from the shed blood of their original wearer. The set of armor Malwynn wore had a hole in the arm and chest where he'd shot two arrows into the wearer, when he was still alive. Malwynn snuck a finger into the chest hole with a sense of satisfaction. He'd already killed one Amaranthine warrior, and was excited to kill more.

"That won't do, will it?" Umaryn asked randomly.

"What? What won't do?" Malwynn responded, his finger falling out of the hole almost shamefully.

"That hole. No front line warrior would wear a suit of armor with a hole in it like that. I can mend it, come here and stand still for me." Umaryn walked over to her brother and squared his body to hers. The two looked strange standing in the decimated village with nothing but a horse, a Gvorn, and burnt rubble around them.

Umaryn took the collar of his armor into her hands and closed her eyes, "Armor from the land of the Purple Queen do you hear me?" She whispered softly to the armor. Malwynn heard no response, but he could tell that his sister did.

"Mmm. You must be in pain then." She said to the armor. Malwynn judged that she wasn't so much responding to the armor, as she was soothing emotions or sensations radiating from it. She seemed as if she was an attentive mother talking to a fitful baby. Umaryn's hands slipped free of the collar and drifted downwards, drawing geometric shapes with the tips of her delicate, yet incredibly strong fingers. Malwynn's mind raced with the patterns her fingers drew, sensing on some strange mystical level that the shapes carried meaning and power, but he failed to comprehend and understand fully what she was doing. As her nails and fingertips dragged back and forth and around she slowly changed their rhythm and dance to a circular motion that ringed the hole in the chest.

She began to whisper again, this time in a similar soothing tone, but full of authority, and resonance, "Let this wound to your spirit be no more. Remember the memory of your perfect self armor, and protect my brother with pride, and my admiration." Malwynn dipped his head down in amazement and watched as the ragged puncture in the armor slowly folded in upon itself like a flower escaping from a full bloom, and resting in the night. Within just scant seconds, the hole was gone, the sheen of the leather had taken on a new brightness, and Malwynn could smell the freshness in the armor return, as if it had literally just been made.

Umaryn suddenly stood up straight, and adjusted the armor roughly on her brother, smiling, "There. Much better.

AT LEAST HE'S NOT ON FIRE

Both holes are fixed too. Best repair spell so far."

Malwynn looked at the armor where the second arrow hole had been. There was absolutely no sign of there ever having been damage, "Wow sister. That's incredible. I will never understand how you do what you do... I am in awe of The Way."

"You and me both. Let's get what we can gather and get moving. The longer we take, the further away they people who did this get."

Despite hours scouring the ruins for food, there was none worth bringing. No morsels of meat, no slices of bread, and certainly nothing sweet to take the bitter taste of ash and death out of their mouths. The twin's bellies cramped and ached from hunger, and once they'd abandoned hope of finding anything to satisfy their need for food, they committed themselves to returning to the hills where they'd left behind the berries.

As Tinder and Bramwell bore them north to the fruit-bearing hills the brother and sister lamented their loss. Umaryn spun her horse about at a rise in the earth and stopped, looking back on the grey waste of New Picknell. What remained of the village at the bottom of the hill looked more like a smudge of memory than a town. Tiny curls of delicate white smoke escaped from underneath massive piles of rubble, heading towards a strange grave far up in the sky.

Malwynn turned his massive Gvorn about and brought it to a rest standing beside his sister. They sat quietly, reins in trembling hands, both watching the smoke rise.

"I wonder what happens to our souls when we die, and don't become undead and aren't set free by the apostles? Is it oblivion? Is it hell? Is it painful?" She asked him, emotionless, seeking some kind of solace.

Malwynn sighed deeply, "I don't know. I hope it's better than the fate of those who die and become undead. We all know that's torment, pure and simple."

"I think dying and not coming back as an undead is almost as good as being blessed and becoming an ancestor spirit. I think it's just restful."

The brother shrugged. "I wish I knew. If it'll help you sleep at night, then I suppose it's like restful nothingness. Like when you wake up and can't quite remember your dreams. Although there's no waking up. No burden of eternal existence as an ancestor, and no rage of the undead. I guess it could be worse."

Umaryn seemed satisfied by that line of logic. She nodded slowly, letting it sway her back to a better mood, "I want everyone who did this to us to die Malwynn. And I don't want a single one of them to be blessed. I don't care if they become undead, but I do not want them to poison the world being spirits. These kind of people can't be allowed to influence the world anymore. They must be removed from existence entirely."

"Erased."

She nodded, "Like New Picknell was."

Oddly enough, no animals had touched the berries. They remained untouched in the finely woven wicker baskets their mother had fashioned when they were children. Both were thankful for the return to the hill not only for the dark blue berries but also for the mementos.

They had precious little evidence now that their family had ever existed. Fleeting memories pulled to and fro in their cluttered and vengeance-clouded minds. Small peeks at blue sky through dark clouds. Holding onto the baskets brought them back to their childhood and back to clear memories that were still untouched by the events they'd just experienced.

They ate a full belly of the rich spoils from the day prior, careful not to eat too much, picked a full bag more, and left heading west towards the rails where they could hopefully find a way north after their prey.

They found tracks about ten miles from the north hill. The hard ground had hoof shaped pockmarks ten paces wide heading northwest, almost the same direction as they were heading initially. Malwynn was not an expert tracker by any means, but he could read the way the dirt was thrown, and could approximately tell their direction, number, and relative speed. Whoever had ridden away from New Picknell had done so at a comfortable pace. The arrogance of might made them feel safe. Malwynn wanted badly to prove their arrogance wrong.

"I think there were about ten of them. No more than twenty. The ground isn't that torn up. Whoever it was moved far north, away from the direct line of the rail from town. I'd bet they rode northwest, and picked up a chartered train. Who has the wealth to charter a train Umaryn?"

"The Purple Queen," she replied.

"Exactly. Makes perfect sense. Charter a small train with an empty freight car, disgorge your mounted warriors, send them south away from the rail so we don't see them get off the train at the rail stop near town, and that's it, the end of New Picknell. They escape the way they came, and reverse the train back to Graben. It's simple. Not even fancy, or hard to accomplish if you bring enough warriors, and necromancers."

"Bastards." Umaryn spat the word.

"What's the name of the last town on the tracks before the border? How far away is it?" Malwynn asked, looking up to his sister from the hard ground. She still sat on Tinder's back.

Her eyes scanned the low rolling hills in every direction, looking for something that might be watching them. She replied, distracted. "Um, I believe it's called... something Fringe."

"Ockham's Fringe. That's it. Dad said it was about a two-day ride away. We are about four hours into that trip. We can head north to there, and use what money we have left to buy a ticket to head north into the Empire. Maybe someone there will have seen the force head north, or know something."

"Perfect. Get on your damn Gvorn and let's get moving. Right now I want to get somewhere I can take a hot bath, that has a hot meal I can enjoy." Umaryn felt her stomach rumble. The berries might have been nutritious, but they were not particularly filling.

"Ancestors bless us, maybe we'll find an elk or deer on the way. Would be a wonderful gift to show we're on the right path."

The two pointed their mounts on a path closely following the trail left behind by the people who murdered their family.

Sense told them to rest their mounts after pushing hard that first day. Malywnn had more experience with horses than his sister, but his determination to move north caused him to forget that despite their size and strength, the creatures they rode needed a break. He persuaded Umaryn to stop at a cluster of fledgling trees in the elbow of a tiny stream to rest that night. It was the only cover in the flat expanse of plains they crossed. The horse was brushed, the Gvorn was brushed, and his thick wool freed of the many tangles under the saddle pad. Malwynn could tell Bramwell and Tinder were happy to be stopped, and they put their long necks low to the ground and ate the sweet green grasses gratefully. He took some satisfaction in his empathy with creatures. It might not be the mystical power that his sister shared with the things created, but it was still something to be proud of.

Umaryn went on at length about how they needed to sleep lightly, and wake with the rising of the sun, but she was blacked out asleep nearly the moment her head was flat on the blanket on the ground. Malwynn watched the rise and fall of her chest and the simple innocence on her face. He'd known her since birth, and he was incredibly thankful he still had her.

As the two moons of Elmoryn, one white, and one red, crept their way up into the dark blue night sky, Malwynn walked away from the shelter his sister slumbered in. He took with him his bow, and the sheaf of arrows he carried for hunting. Hanging from the thickest branch at chest height he'd slung a cotton bag filled with gathered grass and earth. As the night's chill set in, he drew the string of his bow and sent arrow after arrow into the makeshift target. He let the projectiles fly until both moons had disappeared; his fingers were raw, and nearly bleeding. He reminded himself to ask Umaryn to cast her spell of repair on the arrows the next day. He'd dulled their tips.

Like his sister, he was asleep the moment he closed his eyes.

"There you go, all better," Umaryn said, handing Malwynn the quiver filled with freshly sharpened arrows. It'd only taken her half an hour to accomplish the feat with The Way.

"Thank you."

"You know you should've gone to sleep when I did. You're going to be exhausted all day today. It was silly to stay up late shooting arrows in the dark. What if you'd shot Tinder, or Bramwell? What then?" Umaryn asked. Malwynn was taken slightly aback by how much she sounded like their mother. Something about her tone, and her body language.

"I put the target well away from them, as well as you. There was no danger. Besides, we both need to be practicing our fighting skills. I'm good with the bow, but I need to be better."

Umaryn conceded his logic. "I guess if you need to rest we can tie Bramwell on to Tinder and you can flop forward in your saddle. I'll cross my fingers you don't fall off the saddle though. Now that would be funny." She grinned. Malwynn nodded, smiling in return.

After getting their mounts ready to move, filling their water skins, and eating the last of the blueberries, the two left the pleasant little camp and wandered back to the trail they had followed the day before.

Their suspicions were proven quite correct by noon. Under the oppression of the hottest sun they'd felt in days the twins examined the spot at the rails where the tracks became very cluttered and complex, and simply terminated. The prints approached one side of the train rails, and then never appeared on the other side. Whoever had done this had left with all their mounts loaded on a train.

"I guess that solves that mystery," Umaryn said bitterly.

"Indeed. If we push, we can reach Ockham's Fringe by nightfall. Maybe a bit after. Hopefully we can find a few answers there."

The two agreed, and they turned parallel to the rail

tracks, and started to head almost directly north in the direction of Ockham's Fringe, and the Amaranth Empire, home of the Purple Queen.

"Stop," Malwynn said out of the blue. Only an hour had passed since they turned north at the tracks, and the heat of the day was wearing them to the bone. Skin was angry and red, and covered in salty sweat. He peered north towards the horizon, his eyes squinting against the brightness of the yellow sunlight.

Umaryn halted Tinder, "What? What do you see?"

"There's something large ahead, down near that stream. Can you see it? It's big, maybe another Gvorn or something? A wild horse? Any chances the ancestors are smiling on us and sent us an elk?" Malwynn could see a quadripedal creature near the edge of a small stream. Likely the same stream they'd camped at the night prior. The creature was frozen with its head down, like it had just taken a drink from the slow moving water and heard the twins coming. Just upstream from the creature he could see a small wooden bridge for the rails crossing over the water as well.

"It's far too large to be a horse or elk. Oh dear. I think that's a Plains Walker. Look at the front of it. It's got horns, not antlers." Umaryn was surprised.

Malwynn squinted a bit more and shifted where his hand was, better shielding his eyes. Suddenly the creature's form drew into focus. It was huge as his sister said. It was much larger than Tinder, and even bigger than Bramwell. At the shoulder it stood as tall as the twins, just shy of six feet, but its girth was immense. The creature had no head, having only four thick tree trunk sized legs at each corner of its body. From piggish hoof to piggish hoof running the length of its body, the creature was nearly twice the length of Tinder, and probably more. At each end instead of a head or tail, the creature wore two strange natural body parts. A pair of curving horns as large as an Ebonvale warrior's scimitar sprouted forth in a strangely threatening manner. Malwynn was reminded of the wild hogs he and his father hunted several summers back and their brutish tusks. Opposite the pair of tusks were two thick and tough appearing appendages, somewhat resembling a pair of tails, though they moved more like limbs might. From this distance, it was hard to gauge which end was supposed to pass for the head.

"What do we do?" Malwynn asked, suddenly trying to keep his voice low.

"I think they are dangerous. Maybe we should cross to the other side of the tracks and pass that way, far to the west so it can't see us. Best to avoid a fight with a creature twice the size of us and our horses," Umaryn offered.

"I have a Gvorn, you have a horse."

"Fuck you Malwynn you know what I meant. That thing could run us over as surely as the trains that run on these here tracks. Little reason to anger it. Let's just give it a wide berth, okay?" Umaryn said snippily.

"You're right. Let's go."

Changing course due west instead of north, the brother and sister gingerly headed towards the twin rails to cross them. The straightest route had them move slightly closer to the Plains Walker far away at the stream. Umaryn crossed the rails first, guiding Tinder over the minor obstacle with impressive confidence and skill. Malwynn felt it took her no effort at all with the animal.

He did not perform the same task with the same grace. Bramwell and Malwynn had not yet fully bonded, and mount and rider still had many subtle nuances to learn of one another before something even that simple could be managed perfectly. As Bramwell crossed the tracks the very bottom of a hoof struck the iron rail, setting free a resounding metallic ping. Both brother and sister spun their heads back to the Plains Walker, wincing.

The creature's posture had changed. It swayed back and forth, allowing its massive shoulders to feel out the air around it. The creature twisted, pivoted in place, using all four of its legs in a manner neither had seen a creature move in. The legs appeared able to move forward, backward, and side to side with equal ease. Suddenly the creature oriented itself with the two massive curved spikes aimed directly at the top of the ridge where they had frozen.

"Do you think it sees us? Where are its eyes?" Malwynn whispered over a warm and gentle breeze.

The creature answered by lurching forward at them, charging across the grassy terrain directly in their direction.

"Shit! Go! GO!" Malwynn hollered, the ruse of stealth now abandoned fully.

The two kicked hard and sent their creatures bolting forward. Umaryn, already having crossed the rails, was over the loose stone the heavy timbers sat on and was down the ridge and heading as far away as fast as Tinder could carry her. Malwynn's thunderous Gvorn was only a few lengths behind her but his beast wasn't built for speed, simply power. The two sped their animals straight out from the rail as fast as they could, and Malwynn stole a glance over his shoulder to see if the Plains Walker had reached the top of the raised land where the rails were. His stomach reached his feet when he saw all four of its ungainly appearing legs pumping strongly straight down the hill directly on their heels. The Walker had covered the entire distance in only a few breaths of time.

"It's almost upon us! Faster!" Malwynn screamed, this time louder than the first. He watched as his sister's heels dug into Tinder's side and the resulting increase in the creature's speed. He attempted the same on Bramwell, but the creature was already breathing as hard and running as fast as it could. He stole another glance a second later just in time to watch as the creature's massive tusks rammed lengthwise into Bramwell's hind quarter, sending rider and mount sprawling violently into the earth. Malwynn let loose a terrified scream as he fell sideways into the ground, his legs, hips, ribs and shoulders crumpling with horrifying force. Tumbling sideways directly in the air above him he watched as Bramwell utter a whinny and snort, itself spinning end over end, doing a wildly raucous version of what he'd just done himself. Through the stars in his vision and the spinning in his head he watched his brand new mount collide with the earth as he did.

The Plains Walker took several moments to slow itself down to a stop, its incredibly thick muscles working as breaks. Malwynn couldn't force the air into his bruised lungs fast enough to beg his sister for help, so he reached around his body painfully, searching for his bow, and praying to the spirits of all his deceased family members that it wasn't broken by the fall.

The creature took a wide circle to turn back on Bramwell and Malwynn, but when it straightened itself out, it pointed the massive horns menacingly at the nearly senseless pair.

"Mal!" He heard his sister yell panicked from some ways away. He could feel the earth tremble with each of the Plains Walker's steps, as if a tree trunk was being dropped into the ground by one of the legendary Mountain Spirits. The pounding increased in severity as the animal came closer and picked up speed. His sister's scream caused the juggernaut to halt and twist its strange body slightly to the side. It had heard her.

Malwynn was to his knees by then, having gotten the bow off his back. Littered on the ground all around him in the yellowing grass he saw his spilled quiver, over half the arrows broken by the collision with the ground. He saw a single arrow in arm's reach and as quick as his bruised arm could, he drew it, and sent it flying directly between the two horns on the creature. The arrow plunged into the thick hide of the monster far smoother and deeper than Malwynn imagined it would. The skin of the beast looked grey, and was pebbled like stone. He thought it would be tough, but apparently that was not the case. As the creature flinched at the sting of the arrow, he snatched up a second arrow, and let it fly at the same area of its body.

The second arrow plunged almost as far as the first did, stopping nearly halfway in its length. He grinned in exultation as the creature flinched again. What he saw next alarmed him, and stole his moment of glory. The first arrow, sank over a hand's depth into the creature abruptly fell off, as if all of what had penetrated the beast had been simply pushed out from within. The length of the arrow, from feathers to barren tip fell to the ground as if the arrowhead had never existed. Malwynn looked up from the impotent arrow to the creature, and saw it had started to rumble towards him again.

Flanking the creature, Umaryn had dismounted, slapping Tinder to send it away from the battle. She already had her weapon; Chael's hammer up, and was twisting her whole body into the hardest swing she could manage, directly at the rear leg joint of the Walker. Malwynn closed his eyes as he accepted his death approaching him.

It didn't come. Instead he heard Umaryn's powerful grunt of the swing, and the resulting wet snap of the small metal head of the hammer impacting the joint. In his mind's eye the strike to the knee sounded wet, like a mother slapping a pile of her children's wet laundry, yet also much like the breaking of a green tree branch. He wondered what about the animal's nature would make such a strange noise. He had precious time to ponder the mystery though, as the creature staggered sideways, his sister's hammer blow clearly having damaged it. On three powerful legs instead of four, the monster spun itself in a near-perfect circle, and put the side of both of the horns directly into his sister's torso, tossing her through the air ten feet like she was a bale of hay. She screamed in pain and fear for her entire journey through the air, and landed on her ass, flattening her back and head out powerfully against the earth. She lay still while

Malwynn scrambled to find another arrow as the creature turned its attention towards his sister and Tinder, as the horse backed away in fear.

Malwynn drew the bow string and sized up where the creature was vulnerable. In a split second he noticed how the creature was favoring the knee his sister had struck. He hoped strongly that the other joints were equally vulnerable, and sent his arrow into the knee of the leg closest to where he still knelt. The arrow pierced the thick skin of the creature as easily as before, but lodged in something firm very quickly. The arrow could not pass through the joint, for there was too much bone and muscle there, but the projectile stopped in the midpoint, gumming up the tender ligaments, tendons, and stopping the leg's functionality almost completely. Malwynn held his breath as he reached around in the grass hoping that this third arrow wouldn't fall out harmlessly. By the time he'd found another useful arrow, the knee joint was still locked stiff from the arrow.

"Umaryn, get up, we've hurt it!" Malwynn said as he got to his feet. She stirred slightly, the tremendous blow having tossed her consciousness around. Malwynn circled the creature as it hobbled on two good and two bad legs. It was confused now, unsure of where the danger came. The two massive horns swung side to side threateningly, not actually in danger of harming anyone. Mal took a couple quick steps in and flung another arrow into a different leg, missing the joint but piercing through the flesh just below it. The creature jerked to the side again, and suddenly lost the strength to stand. It fell sideways onto the ground, revealing its underbelly.

Malwynn caught his breath as he saw a trench in the stomach of the beast. From what he imagined to be the chest to the crotch there was a mouth running the length of the creature. He hadn't seen the thick skin forming into lips and prehensile feelers that must have been the creature's enormous mouth. It was so wide and long it could have easily lowered itself onto Malwynn or Umaryn, and

AT LEAST HE'S NOT ON FIRE

swallowed them whole. He looked up and saw his sister, limping over to his side, giving the immobilized creature a wide berth.

"Look at this," Umaryn said, hefting her weapon, Chael's hammer up. The hammer's perfectly polished head was bent, deformed, and pockmarked as if it had been immersed in flame and acid. The weapon looked ruined. Umaryn's eyes were filled with tears over the destruction of the weapon she'd hoped to put to good use against the people who had killed her parents. Malwynn watched as her lips trembled and her teeth clenched in anger.

"Maybe you can fix it with The Way?" Malwynn asked, feeling the pain in his stomach and chest rise and fall with his breath. He wondered if the fall from Bramwell had cracked a rib or two.

She nodded, wiping away the tears, "Maybe. How do we kill this damn thing? Where is its head? Where is its heart? Is Bramwell okay? Are you okay?"

Malwynn looked back at his new Gvorn and assessed it. The animal shouldn't be ridden for at least a day, but it appeared to be none the worse for wear. The dead necromancer's mount was a rugged creature. "He'll be okay I think. Although neither he, nor you or I are in any shape to ride any more today. We need rest."

Umaryn reached a hand around to her backside and massaged her lower back. He was right. She would fold to the pain after just a few minutes of trying to ride Tinder. "Agreed. But still, how do we kill this thing? It isn't right to let it suffer like this."

"Your hammer is nearly destroyed from striking it. My arrows had their tips disintegrated and were shunted straight out of its flesh. Anything metal seems to be eaten by the touch of the creature."

Both were quiet for a bit. Umaryn's eyes opened after a bit, full of inspiration, "Help me get a large stone from the stream. I wonder if this thing can handle being beaten by a large rock?"

In fact, the Plains Walker could not withstand being beaten with a large rock. The twins found a stone almost the size of a man's belly on the edge of the stream. The smooth oval-shaped rock was worn from centuries of water flow, and was nearly too heavy for them to lift high. Had they been in a less damaged state it would've been easier, but good fortune was something that had not been in their life for several days. The twins heaved the stone onto the creature's belly multiple times, hitting so the stone would tumble end over end and land on the ground. They were fearful of touching the beast.

A score of these blows and the Walker's breathing stopped. They'd finally ruptured something inside it enough, and freed it from the pain of having three of its limbs ruined.

"I remember talking to Luther about these things at the forge," Umaryn said as the two slumped to the ground, exhausted.

"Yeah?"

"Yeah. Luther said they were a real bane to metalworkers, but were damn good eating. I wonder how we eat this thing?" She asked.

Malwynn could hear her stomach rumble from his seat next to her, "Are you serious? You want to try and eat this thing? It destroyed a bunch of my arrows, and your hammer. How do we gut it? You have a stone knife handy?"

"That's a great idea Mal! Hold on." Umaryn got to her feet with as much energy and enthusiasm as she could muster, given the circumstances. She hobbled her way over to the stream and searched around for several minutes, overturning rocks and using her dagger to dig through the earth. After a good time searching, she came back, holding a rock that only resembled a knife in the loosest possible way. It was perhaps eight inches long, and about as thick as her wrist, and approximately the same sharpness. She had a grin from ear to ear.

"What. The. Hell. Is. That?" Malwynn asked her, his voice dripping with sarcasm and judgment.

Still grinning she held the stone up proudly to him after crossing her legs on the ground next to him, "This is our stone knife. We're gonna keep this around I think. Could be useful down the line."

"I think your fall might have knocked you senseless Umaryn. I think you've gone loony."

Her grin remained for a moment, but then disappeared as she produced a smaller stone from her trouser pocket. With an intensity he'd only seen from her at the forge, she cradled the larger stone and started to hit it with the smaller stone, chipping flecks and bits of rock away, shaping it into a far more knifelike state. After ten minutes of sweat inducing work, she held her new tool aloft; a less dull rock.

"Wow. That's not much different at all," Malwynn said, all the sarcasm from his earlier taunts still dripping in his words.

In complete seriousness Umaryn ignored his tone, "To an artificer my brother, there couldn't be any more difference now." Resting the hard round stone on the ground between her legs Umaryn took the knife stone into her hands fully, and cradled it as if it were a kitten, or precious treasure. She closed her eyes and began to issue forth a chant, a steady repeating of syllables and sounds that formed no words. She caressed the length of what was supposed to be the edge of the blade on the rock as she did this, and Malwynn watched in astonishment as the stone itself seemed to melt at her touch, altering its shape to be straight, and far sharper than he could've imagined.

"The Way. Wow. I didn't think an artificer could use The Way on a simple rock," Malwynn said as she ended her chant.

"This wasn't a simple rock anymore Mal. I spent time hewing it into a tool, rough as it was. I breathed life into it with my effort, and passion to create something out of it. I gave it a small spirit, then used the Chant of Sharpness to persuade the spirit to be a little bit sharper for us, if only for a bit." Umaryn said softly, almost in reverence of the magic she'd just brought to bear.

"I will never understand The Way." Malwynn shook his head.

"You don't have to understand it right now. Right now I want you to get a fire started down near that stream, so we can cook the steaks I'm about to carve out of this thing's ass. Destroy my damn hammer. I'll fucking eat you."

Malwynn got to his feet quickly, sporting his own ear to ear grin.

Umaryn discovered quite a bit about the creature when she dissected it in search of dinner. It had no ears, or eyes. How it navigated the world was lost on her. The Plains Walker's skin was leathery, and supple, but had several strange qualities to it. It had two very different layers. The interior layer was fatty, and resinous, almost like a sheath of cartilage covering the entire body. The exterior layer was very similar to the hide of a cow, or horse, but it was free of hair. Instead, it was covered with visible pores across its entire surface. Umaryn was able to press down on the skin hard enough for the pores to ooze a viscous, almost mucus like substance. The clear fluid did nothing to the stone knife she wielded, but when the substance was placed on her lucky iron nail, the results were startling. It ate away at the metal, corroding it and turning its nature to something more akin to wax, instead of iron.

Within seconds her lucky nail had lost its shape, and was gone forever. A moment later Umaryn kicked the dead creature's body repeatedly out of spite.

The flesh of the Walker was very tough when cooked over the spit Malwynn fashioned. Neither knew if this was the nature of the meat, or if Malwynn was a terrible cook, but it didn't matter, their hunger overpowered any complaints they might've had, the flavor was surprisingly good, and the two gobbled up the dark brown meat as fast as they could, eating ravenously.

They sat together, basking in the glory of their kill, completely sore and miserable for the entire cool evening by the stream. For a few moments, they were able to forget they were orphans. When the train heading from Graben to Daris passed by an hour before the sun fully set, its wheels squeaking and groaning on the iron rails, and its artificer-maintained locomotive spitting a great white puff of steam high into the air, they were reminded bitterly of the reality of their situation.

"Do you understand how much weight this poor Gvorn is carrying for you? And how badly this stinks? Umaryn it's wretched," Malwynn said, clutching his nostrils shut. On the back of Bramwell Umaryn had draped the skin of the Walker. She'd taken the hide off with her stone knife just minutes before, claiming if she could get it to a tanner by day's end, it'd make right fine armor.

"I know Mal, but he's so big. He won't even notice he's carrying it." She pleaded with her brother.

"It weighs three times what I do for ancestor's sake. It's big enough to cover his entire body for his own armor."

Her eyes lit up in genius, "Now that's an idea. Gvorn barding made of Plains Walker leather? We'd be filthy rich Mal. Varrland Marks piled as high as the clouds. Puddings, steak, and fresh breads at our fingertips every minute of every day. Can you imagine it?" She trailed off, clearly imagining it.

"You are insane."

She nodded, suddenly a bit sad, "Yeah I am. The money would never stack that high. All those coins would tip over first."

Malwynn put his face in his hands, giving up. Umaryn climbed up into Tinder's saddle gingerly, testing the bruised and battered muscles that kept her from riding the afternoon prior. She winced but knew the pain would be manageable if they took it slow.

"Ready?" Mal asked, shortening the reins on Bramwell.

"Almost, give me a moment to attend to something," Umaryn said, reaching under the small blanket on Tinder's rump and producing her deformed weapon. Chael's hammer had stopped its wasting away shortly after Umaryn had shown it to Malwynn. It was still a misshaped lump of steel at the end of a warhammer's shaft, a travesty compared to its former glory. Umaryn closed her eyes and lifted the weapon's head close to her mouth, whispering to it, and dragging her fingers across the lines of the oddly shaped blob. Malwynn became uncomfortable watching her cast the spell after a moment more. It seemed too personal, too intimate, and almost sexual. He felt perverted just being nearby, and actually turned Bramwell about to give her more privacy.

After a minute or two of using The Way, she stopped. "Wow. It worked."

Malwynn brought Bramwell about once more and looked at the weapon. Yet again he was amazed at the magic his sister wielded; the weapon was exactly as it had been before the acidic Walker's skin had ruined it. Fully polished and in perfect condition, ready for war.

"Fantastic work."

"Thank you. Remind me again why we aren't wearing our armor now. And why we've wrapped the Amaranth axes in our blankets? I feel very vulnerable without armor handy," She said as she slipped the warhammer back into its resting place.

"As nice as it is to wear decent armor in the wild, I think we'll receive an entirely different welcome in a Varrland town if we ride in wearing armor from the Empire. I think we'll be the ones answering uncomfortable questions. Better to seem forgettable right now," Malwynn answered.

"That's pretty sound reasoning brother. I think I'll keep you around."

"You've got little choice in the matter dear sister. Let's get to Ockham's Fringe. Only one train left today heading into Graben, and I'd like to get there before it leaves."

Brother and sister, battered, bruised and sore, left the corpse of the Plains Walker behind, and headed north to the last town in their home country. It felt eerily similar to walking up to the edge of a cliff to them.

They did not reach Ockham's Fringe in time to catch the last train passing through from Daris to Graben. They knew that when it passed them heading north before they reached the village.

Ockham's Fringe was a traditional Varrlander village. The town proper was larger than New Picknell, nearly three or four times the size by their estimation. Every structure inside the town was encircled by a tall and thick wooden wall reinforced by earth piled against its interior. The wall was sturdy, and was designed to keep undead both out and in should something terrible happen in the village. Most of the buildings inside the sturdy walls were made of brick and mortar, with smooth glass windows framed in iron bars should the undead attempt to get in, or out.

Outside the town's walls the first thing a visitor on the trains would see was the artificer rail station. Far larger than the solitary platform outside New Picknell, this was a building large enough to house a dozen souls waiting for a train in the rain, as well as a platform running along the rails the length of the twin's former home in New Picknell. The roof was covered in expensive slate tile and the building itself formed of brick and mortar. On both sides of the structure sat two rows of large oak trees that had been brought over a long distance and grown to give the building more presence. It was a small icon of the power of the Artificer Guild in a tiny and remote place. Umaryn was in rapture looking at it.

They tied their mounts off outside the building and walked through the wide double oak doors into the main room of the station. To one side was a single window that had a hand painted sign above it reading; PASSAGE TICKETS. On the other side of the window sat a middle aged man with a receding hairline, and slightest touch of gray hair at the temples. He fidgeted with a block of wood and a small but sharp knife as they approached. He sat it down quickly and perked up.

"May I help you?" The artificer asked politely.

"We were looking to buy passage for two adults and two beasts of burden to Graben on the next train," Malwynn asked, trying to feel comfortable and at ease. In reality on the inside he was knotted up with anxiety. This was the first living person they'd spoken to since New Picknell had been destroyed, and Mal felt as if the man knew their plan for vengeance.

"Oh, I'm so sorry. The last train departed about half an hour ago. Would you like to purchase passage on the midday train tomorrow?"

"Yes that'd be fine thank you," Malwynn said back,

feeling a bit more comfortable. He reached to his belt for the small bag of Varrland Marks he kept. It wasn't much, but it was all they had.

"Well we are three quarters of the trip from Daris to Graben here at Ockham's Fringe. That discounts the passage price from 55p to just 13p each. Passage price for two horses is another 5p each. Total, that adds up to 36p. We also take Marks and Crowns, sorry." The artificer couldn't have been from Varrland, despite his notable Varrlander accent. No self respecting resident of Varrland would tell anyone a price quoted in Pieces, and not Marks. Pieces were used in Duulan and Farmington, but not here when Marks were available.

Malwynn smiled and dug through his coin purse. He had a mere forty Marks in the coins minted in Daris left. Spending the money here on the tickets north would leave them nearly broke when they arrived in Graben. The look on Malwynn and Umaryn's faces must've tipped the man behind the window off.

"Is there a problem?" He asked politely.

Malwynn sighed in frustration and met the man's gaze. An urge of desperation struck him, and he gave deceit a chance, "We've got precious little coin left. Our family died in a fire this week, and we're headed north to find family in the Empire. We've only got what was left on our persons right now. We lost everything in the fire."

Umaryn looked to the floor, appearing to fake emotional turbulence. Malwynn saw she was trying to stifle a grin.

"That's terrible. It's made worse that you need to head to Graben as a way to better your lot in life. I'm told it's quite a terrible place, all in all. Are you sure you want to head north? You might be best served by heading south to central Varrland."

Malwynn nodded solemnly, "We couldn't agree more, but we need to be with our family."

The man behind the counter nodded. For the first time Malwynn saw he was wearing the steel gray robes of the Artificer Guild. He hadn't the red trim though, so Malwynn knew he couldn't use The Way. "Well, I could offer you discounted passage if you're willing to do a little work for me."

The twins perked up, and Umaryn followed the prompt, "What kind of work?"

The man smiled in a way that told them they wouldn't like what he was about to say, "The ground near the hitching posts needs to be raked and shoveled free of horse droppings. Also, the gutters along the roof on both sides of the station here are full of oak leaves. I haven't gotten to cleaning them out all summer, and I'm certain when my superiors come through to inspect the station I'll be in trouble for certain."

Neither were fazed by the requests. Their mother and father had asked them to do worse on a daily basis. Malwynn kept poised, and pressed on, "How much can you discount the passage?"

The man with the thinning gray hair mulled an offer over, "I can discount your fares from 13 Marks down to 8 each. That'd be just 26 Marks for you and your sister, plus your horses."

Malwynn felt that was a decent deal, but pushed for more, "Tell you what. How about we rake and shovel the hitching posts, clean all your gutters, and on the way up to Graben, we ride with our animals, and clean out that freight car as we ride?"

"Oh that'd be quite helpful," the man remarked.

"I'd say for all that you charge us 5 Marks each, and let our animals ride for free. After all, we aren't going to be taking up a seat for a full paying customer, and we'd be leaving the train better than when we got on it."

"You drive a hard bargain young man," he replied with a wise smile.

"My father always said guard your coin. He's gone now, but his advice still stands."

The man agreed, taking note of the mention of the father, "Deal. I'll get your tickets, a shovel and rake, and a ladder for you both if you want to start cleaning out the hitching post area."

"I've also a question sir," Umaryn asked quickly.

"Yes?" The man replied.

"Does Ockham's Fringe have a tanner? I've got a hide I need worked into usable leather and was hoping to find a tanner here to do the work for me."

"Oh yes, of course. I can recommend you to an acquaintance of mine. We crafters tend to stick together, you know," The man said with a smile.

The two reached into the window to shake his hand, and turned to head outside. Umaryn waited until they were outside the oaken double doors before leaning in to whisper to her brother, "I didn't know lying came to you so easily."

"Neither did I," Malwynn said, ignoring her accusation.

"Did father actually tell you to guard your coin?" She prodded.

"No. But it sounded like something he would've said."

Umaryn stopped, and her face turned sour, "You shouldn't do that Mal. You shouldn't put words in mom or dad's mouth like that. You can't make your lie more believable by using them. I don't think they'd approve of you using them to lie. It doesn't seem right to me."

Malwynn stopped, his tempter flaring. He had just saved them almost the entirety of their remaining fortune, such as it was, and his sister questioning him in this way was infuriating. He turned to her, ready to rip into her, but when he saw the hurt in her eyes, and on her face, his anger melted away. He thought of his mother, caring, loving, and honest to a fault. He delved into memories of his father, inquisitive, trustworthy, and reliable to a fault. The error of his ways was abruptly clear to him.

"I'm sorry Umaryn. Never again." He vowed.

"Thank you," Umaryn said back softly, and the two wrapped each other up in an embrace that only the grieving can understand.

- Chapter Four -
Conversations

It took far more out of them to rake, shovel, and clean the gutters than either Umaryn or Malwynn realized it would. Their hands covered in redness and growing blisters from the rake and shovel handles, and both their backs sore from standing awkwardly at the top of the rail station's ladder, they headed to the town's twelve foot high gate in the twilight of the day.

Ockham's Fringe was a large enough town to have its own militia force. At the gate were two men wearing a variant uniform of the typical red and white national Varrlander forces, holding spears held high, and wearing short swords on their hips. They were well equipped for a militia in such a small town. All militias in Varrland were by extension members of the national force, but small Ockham's Fringe would very likely never be called on to support anywhere else. It was a virtual certainty if there was war anywhere in Varrland, it would start right at this tall wooden gate, with these spear wielding militia men being the first to fall, or the first to draw Empire blood.

The guards let them pass with no questions. The twins looked physically exhausted, and the guards had watched them at a distance do all the work at the Artificer station. One guard rapped on the thick iron-bound wood of the door, and another guard peered over the top. They exchanged a few words, and the door swung open to let the brother and sister pass. Umaryn, exhausted as she was, still must have looked pretty to the men, for both of them had their eyes on her until the gate closed behind them. Malwynn had forgotten that his sister was actually quite pretty, even when covered in smudges of grime, and favoring a score of sore muscles.

Malwynn slowed Bramwell down to ask a question of the two guards inside the gate, "Is there a decent inn we could get a room at sir? We've need of two beds, a bath, and a hot meal if it's to be had here."

The guards regarded them with skepticism. Strangers were always a source of ill across Elmoryn. It was a dangerous enough place to live when surrounded by people you knew and trusted. Strangers added a whole new dimension. Sickness, aggression, and bad business were always on the heels of new faces. The guards choked down their disdain however, and sent the two tired siblings down a cobblestone main street in search of Howard's Inn and Brewery. Home of the "border's best ale."

The hoped it had the "border's best beds," more than anything. After dropping the Plains Walker's hide off at the town's tanner, and agreeing to split the hide as payment, they made their way to where they'd sleep that night.

The inn keeper was also the bartender at the tavern. He happened in fact to be the Howard the establishment was named after, and showed no signs of the disdain the guards had. He was also in fact quite happy to have them in his business, and seemed even more excited to take their Marks off their hands for their needs. Malwynn and Umaryn left Bramwell and Tinder to Howard's oldest son, and headed inside. The young boy headed off, leading the two animals into the small stable behind the tavern.

"I've just the room for you two. A family suite, the only one in the whole house. It's upstairs, at the end of the hall. There's two small beds separated by a curtain, as well as a bathtub. I'll have my sons start on the pump immediately. We'll get it filled with hot water from the boiler immediately for you. After you both bathe, you come right back down for some rabbit stew, and a stein of my newest ale." Howard was a thick man, with a bulbous belly he'd grown from testing and sampling too much of his own ale. He had ruddy red cheeks and specks of redness all about the tip of his nose. He said all his words with a pipe hanging out one corner of his mouth, and the five customers in the tavern listening intently. He was putting on a show of good service for them. The two headed upstairs after leaving the man six Marks and the remaining slab of Plains Walker steak for everything, dragging their feet the whole way.

Both brother and sister felt rejuvenated after their bath. It was a rare luxury to stay at an inn that had a boiler in the basement, let alone a boiler with connected water pump that could feed fresh hot water straight to a second floor bathtub. Howard's wasn't quite as luxurious as the expensive hotels their mother and father told them about in places like Eden Valley and Farmington, but it certainly was far more than they expected. They washed their clothes in the tub as well as their bodies, rinsing off the fine layer of dust and ash they'd carried with them from New Picknell.

The two wore the only spare clothing they had back down to the tavern to eat that night. Umaryn wore a nightgown that hung on her frame a little loose, and draped low. Malwynn wore loose cotton pants and a sleeveless cotton shirt. They wore their bedclothes, and didn't give a care who thought anything of it.

Fortunately Howard's clientele were not judgmental, in light of Umaryn's cleavage and especially after a large mug of the homebrew. The twins sat themselves at the long, beaten wooden bar and Howard immediately brought them two handmade wooden bowls filled with rabbit stew. The dark bowls filled with hearty stew were emptied twice as fast as the two mugs of ale brought over right after. Everything was delicious, even Howard's brew. Sweet carrots, hearty potatoes, celery still slightly crisp in the broth, and the delicate chunks of rabbit meat were all seasoned delicately, and filled their bellies in a way the Plains Walker meat could not. Their hunger sated, and their minds and moods loosened by the alcohol in the ale, the two grew the courage to ask questions of Howard, and his customers.

"How long have the Amaranth forces been... uh, you know, been coming over the border here Howie?" Mal asked, struggling to get his words closest to the meaning he'd imagined in his head. He hadn't been drunk in some time.

Howard rubbed his belly and tossed a hand towel over his shoulder, "Well that's been happening for longer than I can recall. The Purple Queens have been sending people over the border since my grandfather was a child, and probably longer than that."

"Wunder why?" Umaryn asked, slurring slightly.

"Power, plain and simple. More territory means more wealth. More territory means more folks to do her bidding. This Queen is no different than her mother, and her mother before that. The throne corrupts every daughter who sits in it, pure and simple. You know the old saying about people being cut from the same cloth eh? Well it fits that bloodline perfectly. They are all stamped out of a mold, and as soulless as anything made in that fashion."

"Here here!" Umaryn agreed. To say something or someone was made out of a mold was a powerful insult, especially around the ears of an artificer, or those able to hear the spirits within the things created by hand. Items made of molds, or made in bulk were stillborn of spirit life.

"Any forces cometh through here... lately?" Malwynn asked, his tongue feeling far too fat in his mouth to be saying so many words.

AT LEAST HE'S NOT ON FIRE

A fairly sober patron from a table nearby answered his question, "Son they aren't dumb enough to ride through Ockham's Fringe in a full patrol. They know we'd either ride out to turn them back, or we'd send a message to Daris to summon forces to meet them. I suppose they could put a small army into a few freight trains though, if they found Artificers willing to take the bribe."

The twins turned and digested what he said. They were hoping for the gem of insight that someone had seen the patrol, but judging by the amount of people in agreement with the customer who'd just spoken, that was unlikely.

Another man added to the conversation, "Sometimes on the trains you'll see Amaranth people. You can always tell it's them too. They wear those damn purple robes arrogant as all get out. Once, I even saw one of the sonofabitches with two walking dead on leashes, like pets. Turned my stomach so fast I lost my breakfast. He laughed at me he did. I could've struck him down out of anger and ten men would've helped me burn his body, but I couldn't be sure he wasn't thick with The Way. A necromancer."

"Any of those purple robed riders of late?" Umaryn asked the man. She seemed suddenly more sober.

"Of course. There are always emissaries heading back and forth between Graben and other places all over Elmoryn. Daris is a hub city ya know. You can get to almost anywhere from there, and there's just the one rail line running into the Empire. I wish we could just pay the damn Artificer's Guild to rip up those train tracks once and for all and cut that bitch and her crazies off from the rest of the world."

The chorus of agreement was powerful, and drowned out any chance of a quick follow up question by either brother or sister.

Another patron spoke up, this time a middle aged woman from behind the counter, perhaps Howard's wife, "That just won't work though Carver, and you know it. Not only will Ockham's Fringe dry up like a grape in the sun, but the Artificers won't let a single rail line be harmed. It's their duty, and their belief that those rails are sacred. They pre-date The Fall. They're a symbol of all our pasts, Empire and otherwise."

This time the reaction was more hushed.

"Sometimes we need to forget the past to move on darling. Even if it's painful to do it," Howard said quietly.

Malwynn and Umaryn looked at one another, and let the innkeep's words resound in the silence between them.

Umaryn fell asleep before Malwynn did once again. He envied her ability to shut her mind off so fast at night. Even as small children she could close her eyes and be dreaming in half the time it took him. His mind simply refused to shut off at night. He could hear the tavern slowing down its pace through the floor of their room, and an idea struck him. He could accomplish something quickly, and easily, and then return to try and sleep again.

Mal let himself out of the bedroom quietly, carrying his change purse and what was left inside it for money. It wasn't much, but it was everything they had left. He and his sister's entire accumulated wealth. He hoped it'd be enough for him and sister to accomplish what they needed to do.

When he reached the bottom of the stairs and entered the single roomed tavern filled with wooden beams, the only person left was Howard, still cleaning off tables. He carried a wooden tray filled with clay mugs over to the bar and saw Mal out of the corner of his eye.

"Oy, Mal. Need another drink to get your dreams kick started?" Howard asked.

Mal smiled, "No, I came down to ask a favor of you."

Howard sat another full tray of mugs on the bar counter

AT LEAST HE'S NOT ON FIRE

as his wife carried the first away to the back room of the bar to be washed. Left alone again, Malwynn walked over to the bar, and emptied the coin purse's contents. He slid the coins with deft but sore fingers into their values, and quickly counted what his entire worth was.

"I've got eighteen and a half Marks left in my pocket Howard," Malwynn said, looking at the map with very serious eyes.

"A good amount of coin for the average man, well done son. Your father's proud, I'm sure."

Mal fought off the surge of emotion at the mention of his father. He took a deep breath, and continued, "Do you have Crowns here?"

Howard let loose a short laugh, "Crowns? Yeah I've got some. You want Crowns? They're almost worthless you know? You can spend them here, and in the Empire, and that's it. I mean I've heard some places honor their value, but that's few and far between."

Malwynn nodded, knowing the truth in Howard's words.

"Wait a second. Which direction is that train going you're headed out on tomorrow? What are you and your sister planning?" Howard asked, suddenly serious, and worried for the young people in his care, even if only for the night.

Malwynn pushed the coins toward Howard as his response, "Eighteen and a half Marks Howard. Can you give me Crowns for this?"

"The Empire will chew you two up and spit you out, you know? It's the place where dreams go to die. You should get on that southbound train in the morning and forget about all this." Howard stared at Malwynn with cold eyes. Mal saw some kind of sadness in Howard's eyes, and had to look away.

"Howard, we need Crowns please. If you can't do it, I understand, but our path is already laid for my sister and I." Malwynn summoned the strength to look the old man in the eye again.

Howard looked very unhappy with that reply, but turned and reached under the counter, rummaging a bit before finding a small wooden box. He opened the thin lid and then dumped out the contents. Dozens of metallic coins with a purple sheen spilled out. He started to count them out, but stopped abruptly.

"Just take them all. You're going to need them where you're going."

"Thank you Howard. My sister and I will remember you. One day I'll settle this debt, you've my word," Malwynn extended his hand and Howard took it.

"You own me nothing. Take care of yourself Malwynn, and your sister."

Malwynn let go of Howard's hand, and filled his empty coin bag with the tainted purple coins of the tainted Purple Queen.

"The tanner says the hide will be ready in a week for me to work. I think I'll make it into some kind of studded leather, but nicer than this Amaranth armor we have. That stuff is decent, but I think I can make better," Umaryn said as the twins rode out the gate towards the Artificer rail station. Both were wrapped from head to hip in blankets they bought from Howard. In truth Howard let them have the blankets when Umaryn asked for them, but Malwynn left two Crowns on the table in the room they'd rented as remittance. He already felt in debt enough to the man.

The two were wrapped in such fashion because underneath the blankets they wore the Amaranth armor. Fearful of the eyes of the Ockham locals, they wanted no part of being seen wearing the armor. So instead, they suffered the midday summer heat wrapped in wool blankets. They sweated profusely.

The gate guards bid them farewell with more enthusiasm than they'd greeted them with the night prior, and the twins made their way to the platform. Two artificers were on the raised stone platform, taking tickets and managing the handful of people getting on the train. At each end of the train and spread along its length on the ground were numerous Guild warriors. Like their grey robed leaders the security forces wore light plate armor fashioned from steel, and enameled in the same shade of grey as the robes of the Guild. The Artificers employed hundreds upon hundreds of warriors to ride with the trains as they crossed the wild expanses between towns, villages, and cities. It looked to Umaryn that only five people would be boarding train, including them. Bramwell and Tinder were hitched off the platform near a ramp that led up to the freight car they'd be riding in. The brother and sister went up to the artificer taking the tickets so as to board the train.

The man taking the tickets was tall, a full hand higher than the duo. He was thin, and wore the grey hooded robe of the Artificer Guild. Malwynn felt a little nervous as he looked at the blood red trim that advertised to all those gathered that this man could wield The Way. Mal was afraid to lie suddenly.

"Sir, we've tickets for the midday Graben departure," Malwynn said, handing the tall man the scripts of paper detailing the conditions of their journey.

The tall man had short, well trimmed bright blonde hair, and eyes almost as bright blue as theirs. He scanned the two slips and started shaking his head negatively, "I'm sorry, but I can't allow you to ride with your animals. That's against Guild policies."

The twins looked at him incredulously. Their bad fortune seemed never ending. Just as they were about to let in on a tirade to save their trip, the tall blonde Artificer added to the conversation.

"The passenger cars are nearly empty today. I can simply allow you to ride with the passengers. When we arrive at the Graben rail yard, you can leave the train and clean the car, as per your agreement with the station here. I hope that's acceptable." The Artificer watched as their expressions changed from exasperation to gratefulness.

Umaryn nearly embraced the man, "Oh that'll be fine sir. Sorry for our response, we've had a quite difficult week, and we thought you were about to make it much worse."

He nodded, seemingly understanding, "The Guild made an agreement with you to ride this train. We'll honor that agreement, though clearly not in the way you'd expected. I'm sorry if I gave you the wrong impression."

"It's alright. Quite fine really," Malwynn said.

The blonde Artificer smiled again, "Enjoy your trip. Despite what everyone says, the trip north to Graben can be very breathtaking."

The twins nodded, gathered what they needed from the saddle bags of their mounts, and boarded the trains, still wrapped in their blankets, and still sweating heavily in the north Varrland sun.

Once inside the train they shed the blankets. Normally leather armor is uncomfortably warm when the weather is hot, but removing the blankets made both of them feel as if they were running practically naked through their parent's backyard. Air flowed into the seams and sleeves of the leather and allowed their skin to breathe once more.

Wiping the sweat from her brow, Umaryn looked back and forth to the two passenger cars they had to choose from, "Which one?"

"Um, this one I suppose," Malwynn chose at random,

and the two slid open the finely crafted car door. After they walked by the lone grey guard inside the door, they assessed where to sit.

The car was long, likely fifty feet from where they stood to the front door that led to the locomotive powering the train. The seats and couches were old plush leather dyed a rich green, and the woodwork a rich cherry. Inlaid into the fine carvings were intricate laces of brass and tin, giving the compartment an ancient, and classy feel. Umaryn wondered if this was one of the rail cars that pre-dated The Fall.

The seats were arranged in two sections. Running the entire length of all four sides of the car were the green leather seats. In the center of the car, cutting the compartment in half were two more seats, almost creating two entirely separate areas to sit in. The closest section of seats had six souls resting in it. At first glance it looked to be two families, both reasonably well-to-do, and both with a single younger child. Alone in the far end of the other section of seats sat a lone, tall figure.

Almost alone, that is.

The tall figure was garbed head to toe in a rich purple hooded robe that obscured his face. His hands were deathly white and the skin tight and shrunken. His nails were vaguely yellowed and a bit too long, giving them a sinister appearance. Sitting to his left and right were two zombies.

The undead were both large males wearing simple trousers and plain white shirts. Their flesh was grey and sunken, the rot of death arrested through The Way. Both wore no signs of a violent death, though they were both in their prime. Malwynn and Umaryn each felt their stomachs twist and churn looking at the drained expressions on the faces of the deceased men. Sitting just a few feet away was pure heresy against the ancestors. Around their necks they wore purple ribbons that supported a purple medallion, signifying that they were undead in the service of the Purple Queen. That could only mean in some fashion that the purple robed man directly served the Queen.

Malwynn debated where to sit in an instant. If they crowded into the nearest section with the two families, the entire journey would be cramped and uncomfortable. They would also be tipping their hat to the robed man that they were potentially afraid to sit near him. Malwynn felt the best course of action was to appear confident, and wear their armor like a soldier of the Amaranth Empire would, and sit near the man who they so badly wanted to stay away from.

Malwynn walked past the families, Umaryn at his side with purpose, intentionally seeming disrespectful to their presence. Not one of the six family members looked up to make eye contact as they passed. He reached the two green leather couches that sperated the train's space and addressed the robed figure sitting at the end of the train, "Sir is this seat taken?"

Malwynn's heart froze solid when the hood of the purple man titled up ever so slightly, allowing the eyes covered in shadow underneath enough of an angle to look directly at him. Malwynn couldn't see the face of the figure through the blackness, but he heard the voice loud and clear, "No. Please rest soldier."

The voice was chilling. The tone was low, and sounded as if it began deep in the belly of the man inside the robe, and rattled upwards and out, wheezing through a missing nose in a baritone that seemed to emanate from beyond death. It also had a strange whimsical quality to it, striking Malwynn in a way he couldn't describe. Both he and his sister kept their faces stone-like, and took up seats on either side of the rail car.

It would be a very long seven hour trip.

The man on the platform had exaggerated the beauty of

the Amaranth Empire's terrain greatly. Looking out of the windows in their rail car the only thing they saw for the first four hours of the train ride was flatness. Impossible flatness as far as the eye could see. The only hint of a change in the world was the faint irregularity of hills or mountains far to the north, very far away. As the afternoon began to wane and the sun dipped down close to the horizon the clouds darkened, and thickened. It seemed to Umaryn that the world had been split in two; the flat ground on the bottom, and the dark grey rolling bulges of a storm head moving to the southeast above. She wondered if the storms had anything to do with the presence of such evil in the Amaranth Empire.

"I'm looking forward to seeing the Snake Ridge Mountains again. It's been many weeks since I've laid eyes on them," the purple robed man said unexpectedly. The hair on the back of her neck stood on end at the low raspy voice. Umaryn looked across the car to Malwynn, seeking his support, but his head had tipped back, and he had drifted into deep sleep. She was on her own for this exchange.

"Couldn't agree more," she said confidently.

"What's your name soldier?" He asked her.

She couldn't think of a reason not to offer her real name, "Umaryn sir."

"No last name Umaryn? Strange." The robed man uncrossed and re-crossed his legs. She watched as his fine black leather boots slid in graceful movement. It didn't help his aura of fear any, she thought.

She nodded, as if she'd heard that before. She had. "Our father said taking his last name was a disrespect to our mother, and that it would be better for our personal legacies if we earned a last name from those we encountered."

"Our father you say? The other soldier is your brother then? I suspected as much, the family resemblance is there."

Umaryn felt her worry creep slightly higher again. She did not want this man to know Malwynn was her brother. Unfortunately, the man had already devoured any chance she had at maintaining that secret, "Yes. His name is Malwynn."

"Malwynn and Umaryn the soldiers. Interesting that your mother and father would allow both their children to join the Queen's army. Most parents only allow a single child to join. Did your parents not care for you as much as other parents do?" The robed man asked her in a tone that nearly caused anger in her. He was baiting her, testing her patience and self control. She didn't fall for the trap.

"We are two of three children. Our parents needed the income both my brother and I working provided. This is our way of helping to pay them back." Her words were the truth. In New Picknell both she and Malwynn worked to help support the family.

"Ah. Duty to family. Something I haven't experienced in some time. I focus on my duty to the Queen now." He said, sounding somewhat judgmental. Umaryn felt her story had convinced him. She remained silent, hoping the man would leave her be.

"You're from Graben then?" He said. Her hopes of being left alone were dashed.

"Only just recently. My brother and I actually hail from a very tiny village near the border with Varrland. We've just visited home, that's why we're heading back to Graben." Umaryn felt a surge of confidence. She had no idea she could lie so easily to someone so dangerous.

"Small village life seems so pointless. I maintain that the military should just roll up all of these little villages and bring them to Graben. Keep all the populace in one place that's easy to control. Does your village produce anything of value Umaryn? What validates its existence?" The thin figure leaned in towards her in an inquisitive way, clearly wanting to hear someone he deemed as lesser than he share logic.

Umaryn wasn't sure if she should agree with him, or argue her point. She was swimming in dangerous waters. "Well sir, I don't know what someone of your station would deem valuable. We don't mine, nor do we produce lumber, but we do have multiple farms that produce a fair share of food. We grow more food than we eat, and we send our surplus to the Queen. I imagine the Queen's army appreciates eating meals."

He sat back in the plush green leather couch and chewed on her words, "I imagine they do appreciate eating. Of course we could simply kill them and reanimate them all as undead. Then we'd need no food at all."

"We'd still need to replace their losses in battle. That means having babies, and growing them up to adults. There will always be a need for farms and food in the Empire sir. No amount of Necromancy can change that, no disrespect intended."

The robed figure chuckled evilly, "None taken Umaryn with no-last-name. I enjoy your wit and intelligence. I suspect you'll rise through the ranks of the Queen's army readily."

"Thank you sir." She tipped her head in deference, and appreciation. She was strangely flattered by the scary figure's compliment.

The robed figure went silent for a time.

When Malwynn awoke some time later, the train was running along the foothills of the Snake Ridge Mountains. Amaranth was a wide nation, many thousands of miles across from east to west. It was cut into three pieces by two large mountain ranges. The eastern mountain range, nearest to the Realm of Duulan was called the Giant's Back Mountains. Elliot had told his children that the summits along the Giant's Back were the highest peaks in all of Elmoryn.

The Snake Ridge Mountains were nowhere near as tall, though they were much longer. It would be a very long trip indeed to span the length of the spine of the range, and the city they were headed towards was perched against the cliffs running alongside of them. The rails heading towards Graben were less than two miles from the edge of the mountains, and the location offered a view of the mountains that lived up to the Artificer's claims. This was a natural beauty that neither Malwynn nor Umaryn had ever set eyes upon.

"The majesty of the Snake Ridge Mountains Malwynn," the robed figure said menacingly. Malwynn sat up abruptly, unaware he was being watched. His mind raced trying to figure out how the daemon at the end of the car knew his name. His question was answered with a wave of the eerie figure's hand. He pointed a bony finger at Umaryn, answering his question. She shrugged ever so slightly, trying to convey the entire conversation he'd slept through.

"Yes. They're quite the thing." Malwynn struggled to gather his wits. He'd only been awake a few seconds, and wasn't prepared to have a conversation with someone so alien, so... un-preferable.

"Your sister here says you hail from a small town. How has life in Graben treated you? Quite the change from small village life, yes?" Malwynn felt the questions were heavier than the words used to compose them revealed. He was skeptical of what the man was actually asking.

"Oh, it's different, that's for sure. However, we're kept busy, and there's little time to dwell on silly things."

Malwynn could swear the figure smiled under his black hood, "True words."

Malwynn formulated a plan, and after a minute of watching the ridges and crests of the massive mountain chain pass, he launched his first question at the spooky passenger, "Might I ask your name my lord? You appear to know mine."

The hood moved slightly, indicating a nod, "Your sister

was polite enough not to ask the name of a man well above her station."

Malwynn smiled, "My sister was always the more polite one. I'm far more direct."

"I see this. Both aptitudes have their use thankfully. I shall grant your meager request Malwynn with no-last-name. You may call me Inquisitor Dram Sorber."

Malwynn's blood ran cold. Inquisitors of the Queen held tremendous power in the Empire. They served as spies, magistrates, executioners, and most were powerful users of The Way. This man was potent indeed. "You're skilled in The Way aren't you? A necromancer?"

The hood tilted to the side slightly, "Is it that obvious Malwynn? Does my power radiate from my body like heat comes from the sun? Can you feel my power?" Malwynn knew the man's words were intended to intimidate, and his knowledge of Dram's goal caused the attempt to fail.

"No. I merely made the connection with your robes, and the presence of your... escorts." Malwynn waved his hand casually at the two zombies sitting on each side of the Inquisitor. Malwynn suddenly noted the strange smell of them. Like spices scattered on rotting meat.

Dram leaned back and looked to the twins, assessing them both. Umaryn tried to remain neutral, and kept her gaze on her brother. "Well as you've assessed, I am indeed one of the Queen's Guild Necromancers, as well as an Inquisitor. I'm quite busy you see."

Malwynn leaned back in his own couch and nodded in false approval. So much of his body wanted to draw his dagger from his belt and leap across the car to drive it up under the chin of the man near him. Whether or not Dram had anything to do with the death of his family, and the destruction of New Picknell, he felt this man deserved to die. His title alone warranted execution. Malwynn showed none of this, and continued on with his friendly and respectful demeanor, "It's quite the pleasure to meet you Inquisitor. I'm sorry if my blunt nature has offended you in any way."

"I'm amused by your natures Malwynn and Umaryn. Most citizens are petrified to even be near an Inquisitor. It's a pleasant change of pace to find anyone willing to strike up conversation. They are all afraid I'll pass summary judgment on them, and have them put to death."

"Have you done that Dram? Have you had people put to death?" Umaryn asked.

"Well young lady, I am an Inquisitor. We didn't earn our reputation by not putting people to death." Dram laughed slowly, and all the color drained from the twin's faces.

Malwynn and Umaryn struggled to stay focused as they waited at the bottom of the wooden ramp that led to the freight car Bramwell and Tinder rode on. Graben was an impressive city, far larger than anywhere they'd ever been, and its startling geography had them captivated. Graben was a city divided in half, albeit in a strange fashion.

The city rested flush against a massive cliff in the Snake Ridge Mountains. At the base of the cliff was an area Ellioth had called the Low City. Squat timber homes and buildings spread out from the side of the cliff like an urban stain on the earth. Hundreds upon hundreds of structures were arranged along shoddy dirt roads for hundreds of yards. The ripe stink of human waste and dirty animals filled the air, thick and pungent. Where they stood in the Low City, on the very outer edge was the Artificer Guild rail yard. Unlike the tiny rail station in Ockham's Fringe, this structure was an edifice, dedicated to the Guild as well as the Queen. It rose many stories high, and was chiseled out the grey granite that formed the bedrock of the Snake Ridge Mountains. Columns, domes, intricate carvings and scrollwork, and the ever present color Purple made the building seem enormous, ominous, and cold. Where they stood at the base of the platforms gave them a view of the city unlike anyplace they could've imagined.

Cut into the face of the cliff and running the entire width and breadth of the Low City were doors and windows, indicating that there were homes and businesses entrenched within the stone cliff itself. Near the very center of the Low City and carved into the cliff was a perfectly rectangular space that slid upwards into the mountain until it opened up to the sky at the top of the cliff, well over a thousand feet above the land they stood on. In the channel carved from the cliff two platforms moved up and down side by side in a balanced dance. Both platforms had a footprint larger than their family home in New Picknell, and one rose at the same speed that the other fell. The twins could see people, wagons, horses and even a Gvorn or two on the platforms. From this distance they could see massive chains powering the lifts, but could not discern what controlled the mechanics. Umaryn suspected the Artificers Guild was involved.

At the top of the giant cliff there was a second city. They knew it to be called the High City, the home of Graben's political and military elite. On many window sills, and lining the streets they could only barely see, they saw the tiny purple flowers that gave the Empire its name. Each home in the upper city was carved directly into the face of the mountain, and they were all grand monuments. The smallest palace carved into the mountain on the level of the High City was two stories tall, and beyond beautiful. The stature of the owners of these homes could be gauged by their opulence, by their size and the amount of carvings etched into their faces.

Despite all their independent beauty and character, none could hold a candle to the palace of the Purple Queen. The terrain at the top of the cliff could not have been parallel to the face, for the palace was set further back from the edge than the other residences. The cliff carvings outlining the palace reached up high, at least ten floors higher than the next largest home in the High City, and the detail and grandeur was unmistakable, and oppressive. Sinister gargoyles flanked by intricate pillars decorated the stone the entire length and width of the palace. Intermixed in, tall statues of winged men and women spread their arms in a benevolent gesture, likely meant to lure the populace into believing the resident of the palace was kind, and caring.

No Queen of the Amaranth Empire was kind, or caring.

"I find myself staring at it every time I return too," Dram said from the platform above them. Mal and Umaryn shook the distraction from their eyes and turned to him. He towered above them even more than before, flanked by his two undead pets.

"There is something special about it," Umaryn said before her brother said what she knew he wanted to say.

"Indeed," Dram returned, his face still shrouded in blackness under his purple hood. The six people on the train had already left. They practically ran away from the train and Dram's entourage. Despite being in such a massive city, they felt very alone in his presence. As they shared their moment of strange silence, one of the Artificer Guild's laborers led Bramwell and Tinder down the ramp. Dram's eye line dropped from the cliff down to the animals as they were brought to the twins. Tinder immediately nuzzled Umaryn as she took the reins from the laborer. Bramwell was slightly less affectionate.

"Quite the creature you have there Malwynn. Majestic and strong," the Inquisitor said.

Malwynn smiled, truly appreciating the compliment, "Thank you Inquisitor Sorber."

"I find it interesting that a young man from a tiny village who had to join the Queen's army to support his family would be able to afford such a creature."

Brother and sister exchanged glances at one another. Their story was beginning to unravel. Malwynn looked up at the robed nightmare, and tried to piece their cover back together, "Bramwell here was taken from a Varrlander we killed while on patrol a few weeks ago. He had strayed into Empire territory, and we took care of matters."

"Hm. Well done then I suppose," Dram said, clasping his bony hands in one another at his waist. He turned to walk away, and then stopped long enough to utter a single statement that sent the pits of their stomachs below the hard Amaranth earth.

"I find it curious that your Gvorn looks almost identical to one a close associate of mine had." Dram spun on his heels and took his two undead cohorts away, gliding effortlessly across the slate gray stone of the rail platform.

"It's time to get dirty my friends," said the blonde Artificer from behind them. They turned to face him. He rested a wheelbarrow filled with all manner of tools at their feet, smiled, nodded, and left them.

Two long sighs later, they each took a tool, and got to work.

- About The Author -

CHRIS PHILBROOK is the creator and author of *Adrian's Undead Diary* as well as the popular webfiction series *Elmoryn* and *Tesser: A Dragon Among Us*.

Chris calls the wonderful state of New Hampshire his home. He is an avid reader, writer, role player, miniatures game player, video game player, and part time athlete, as well as a member of the Horror Writers Association. If you weren't impressed enough, he also works full time while writing for Elmoryn as well as the world of Adrian's Undead Diary and his newest project, Tesser; A Dragon Among Us.

- Find More Online -

Check out Chris Philbrook's official website **thechrisphilbrook.com** to keep tabs on his many exciting projects. Sign up for his email newsletter to stay informed about the latest developments and special announcements, or follow Chris on Facebook at **www.facebook.com/ChrisPhilbrookAuthor** .

Don't miss Chris Philbrook's smash hit: *Adrian's Undead Diary*. Follow the exploits of Adrian Ring in this epic eight-book series as he searches for meaning, survival, and hope in a world ravaged by the dead. Visit **adriansundeaddiary.com** to learn more about Adrian's world. Available in print, Kindle, and online.

Follow Chris Philbrook's latest epic series as it unfolds in *Tesser: A Dragon Among Us*. Meet Tesser, the Dragon. He who walks in any form, and flies the skies free of fear. He has slept for millennia, but now he has awoken in a world ruled by human hands, where science has overshadowed even the glory of old magic. Follow Tesser as he seeks to understand why he slept for so long, and where all the magic has gone. Visit **adragonamongus.com** to learn more.

Read more by author Chris Philbrook in *The Kinless Trilogy*. Explore Elmoryn, a world of dark fantasy where death is not the end. The story begins in *Book One: The Wrath of the Orphans*, available in print, Kindle, and online. Visit **elmoryn.com** to learn more about Elmoryn, view concept art, and much more.

Can't get enough of AUD?

Visit the School Store at **adriansundeaddiary.com** for stickers, hats, and a wide variety of awesome shirts!

Made in the USA
Middletown, DE
08 July 2024

56798030R00130